GONE AGAIN

Doug Johnstone (@doug_johnstone) is the author of four previous novels, most recently *Hit and Run* (2012), described by Ian Rankin as 'a great slice of noir' and by Irvine Welsh as 'a grisly parable for our times'. Writer-in-residence at the University of Strathclyde from 2010–2012, he is also a freelance journalist, a songwriter and musician, and has a PhD in nuclear physics. He lives in Edinburgh.

www.dougjohnstone.wordpress.com

Praise for Doug Johnstone:

'Doug Johnstone hits YOU and then HE runs, and you never catch him until the last word of the last sentence. Cracking stuff.' Alan Glynn on *Hit and Run*

'A hugely atmospheric thriller soaked in the spirit of life . . . sip and savour.' *The Times* on *Smokeheads*

'A counter clockwise, state of the nation rock'n'roll tour which captures where we're at better than any modern novel I've read.' Irvine Welsh on *The Ossians*

'A seductive and thrilling evocation of what lurks beneath the surface of small-town Scotland – or indeed small-town any-where.' Christopher Brookmyre on *Tombstoning*

Gone Again

DOUG JOHNSTONE

ff

faber and faber

For Aidan and Amber

First published in this edition in 2013
by Faber and Faber Limited
Bloomsbury House
74–77 Great Russell Street
London WC1B 3DA

Typeset by Faber and Faber Limited
Printed and bound by CPI Group (UK) Ltd, Croydon, CR0 4YY

The right of Doug Johnstone to be identified as author
of this work has been asserted in accordance with Section 77
of the Copyright, Designs and Patents Act 1988

A CIP record for this book
is available from the British Library

ISBN 978–0–571–29660–6

FSC
www.fsc.org
MIX
Paper from
responsible sources
FSC® C101712

2 4 6 8 10 9 7 5 3 1

I

Mark struggled to keep himself steady. Sharp gusts of wind were nudging his camera all over the place and the spray coming off the sea was probably eating away at the lens casing. He should change to a longer lens for this shot but he didn't want to risk getting salt into the electronics.

He looked out to sea. Rough grey swells were chopping up the firth, where a coastguard speedboat was zipping and turning, trying to guide the whales towards open water. Black fins darted and dipped, too many to count properly, but at least forty. The pilot whales circled and crossed each other in a strange movement that might've been mesmerising if Mark wasn't on a deadline.

He flicked back through the shots he'd already taken. There were a few that the paper could use, but he wanted something better. He checked his watch. Five minutes to deadline but he probably had a bit longer, the picture desk was always hustling him.

He adjusted the feet of the tripod in the sand. A surge of wind made him spread his weight to steady himself and the equipment. Up to 70 mph they said on the news this morning, and this was supposed to be spring, almost summer.

He looked through the viewfinder. He needed to get a picture of the whales spyhopping, that was the money shot. He'd listened to a marine biologist being interviewed on the beach earlier. Apparently it was very common behaviour for pilot whales. Sticking their heads above the water like meerkats and having a nosy around, especially at nearby boats. He could do with one of them taking a peek right now. But all he could see was a mess of fins rising and sinking, the occasional tail flick, but nothing spectacular, nothing that would make the front page.

The biologist had said the potential stranding might have to do with the wind somehow messing with their navigation. Either that or pollutants, or magnetic fields, or sonar. The guy had no clue, basically. One thing he did say was that pilot whales were always doing this, and the strong social bond meant if one beached, they all did. Mass suicide.

He began uploading the shots to the picture desk through his phone, his eye back to the viewfinder, legs spread and feet planted in the sand.

'Come on, spyhop, you sods.'

Nothing. It was as if the whales didn't want to be front-page news. He clicked away anyway, getting the best action shots he could. Got a well-framed picture of the coastguard boat with a guy at the prow and a couple of dorsal fins nearby, spray from the waves adding depth. He took a couple of quick shots of a seagull hovering above an emerging back. But no spyhopping.

The pictures had uploaded. He raised his head to look around. Worth getting a few background snaps, you never know.

A small group of people hugged the shoreline of Portobello beach, huddled in against the ferocious wind, all peering at the whales a hundred feet out to sea. Sand lifted off the surface of the beach and swirled into everyone's faces. Mark dreaded to think what it was doing to his Canon. He took a few pics of the crowd, they might get used if the story ran long, but probably not. He was on shift anyway so it didn't matter, he got paid his pittance either way, but it was always nice to see your work in print, even if it was only the *Edinburgh Evening Standard*.

A couple of people in the crowd were pointing at the firth. He turned to see a whale with its whole head clearly out the water looking straight at the shore. He spun the camera back and snapped, but by the time he got it focused the whale had disappeared back into the churning wash.

'Shit.'

His phone went. It would be Fletcher on the picture desk getting on his back for better shots. He kept his eye at the viewfinder and his finger on the shutter release as he answered the phone.

'That's all I've managed to get so far,' he said.

'I'm sorry?' It was a woman's voice.

He straightened up. 'Hello?'

'Is that Mr Douglas?'

'Yes.'

'Nathan's dad?'

His stomach lurched. 'Yeah, that's right. What is it, is Nathan OK?'

'He's fine. This is Mrs Hignet from the office at Towerbank. It's just to say that no one has come to pick Nathan up from school, that's all, and we were wondering if there was a problem of some kind.'

'I'm sorry, my wife was supposed to pick him up today, I'm working.'

A shudder of wind rocked him as he gazed out to sea.

'I see. Well, Nathan's mum hasn't shown up,' Hignet said. 'Could you come and get him, please? This sort of thing isn't really acceptable, you know.'

'Of course.' Mark looked at his watch. His deadline was past now anyway. He turned and looked along Porty Prom. He could see the school from here, it wouldn't take long to pack up and hoof it over, ten minutes tops. 'I'll come and get him straight away. I'll be there in five minutes.'

'Very good.' Hignet sounded like a real old battleaxe. 'But Mr Douglas, please don't let this happen again.'

Mark raised his eyebrows but kept his voice level. 'Of course not. Sorry.'

He hung up and began packing his gear away, trying to make sure there was no sand anywhere. Pointless in this wind. Camera into the case, lenses packed away, tripod folded and telescoped.

As he crouched over the camera case, he spotted something. Amongst the scattering of stones and shells on the sand there was a small piece of something opaque. Sea glass. He picked it up and stroked the edge of it with his finger. It was the size of a fifty-pence piece and pear-shaped, light blue-green, one of the more common colours. Not that sea glass was common on this beach. Nathan's collection only ran to five pieces so far, that was in six years of beach walking. Mark turned it in his hand, feeling the smoothness against his skin, the glass tumbled and worn by sand and waves, wearing its experience on its surface for all to see. This would make a nice addition to the collection, and Mark smiled at the thought. He slipped the glass into his pocket.

He heard a noise from the small crowd at the water's edge

and looked up. They were pointing at the sea again. He sighed and turned. Two pilot whales, heads held stationary above the waves, looking inquisitively around. Front-page material. Shit.

He got his phone out and made a call. Straight on to voicemail. Maybe she was in the car on her way to school. Stuck in tramworks traffic, most likely.

'Hey, honey, it's me. Where are you? I just got a call from the school saying you haven't picked up Nathan. I'm working at the beach anyway snapping these whales, so I'll head along the prom to get him, OK? See you back at the house.'

He began the heavy trudge through the sand up to the prom, heading for Towerbank, lugging all his gear like a packhorse.

2

Towerbank was a crumbly Victorian block with clanky plumbing, poky windows and not enough rooms. Mark headed for Nathan's classroom, hoping he might still be in there with Miss Kennedy. Better to face her than the old matrons in the office. He passed a large mural on the way to 2B, all about the wonders of the sea. Maybe they'd be painting in dozens of beached pilot whales soon.

He knocked on the door and went in. Miss Kennedy was sitting with a pile of marking, Nathan clicking the mouse at a computer. The forgotten son with the irresponsible parents.

Miss Kennedy looked up. She always made Mark feel so old. Late twenties, black bob, short skirt, cute smile. Jesus. He tried to remember his own primary teachers, pictured a string of ancient, stocky madams with industrial bosoms.

'I'm really sorry,' he said.

Miss Kennedy gave a sparkly laugh. 'No problem.' She turned to Nathan. 'We've just been chilling out, haven't we?'

Nathan kept his eyes on the computer screen and his hand on the mouse.

'Yeah,' he said.

Mark looked at him and felt all the usual parental craziness in a brief rush – pride, worry, love, heartbreak and pain. He went over and tousled the boy's mess of fair hair. Nathan's skin

6

was pallid against the garish red uniform, his green eyes so much like Lauren's. He was playing a platform game to do with healthy eating, collecting fruit and dodging burgers and sweets.

'Come on, Big Guy, let's go home,' Mark said. 'Get out Miss Kennedy's hair.'

'Awww,' Nathan said, but he dragged himself from the computer willingly enough.

Mark ushered him towards the door and turned back. 'I'm so sorry, it won't happen again.'

Miss Kennedy waved this away.

'My wife was supposed to pick him up, I don't know where she's got to.'

'It's fine.'

Outside the door, Mark helped Nathan on with his coat, zipping it up for him to save time. 'It's blowing a gale out there.'

'Where's Mummy?' Nathan said.

'Good question.'

Mark got out his phone and called again. Voicemail. He didn't leave a message.

'Daddy?'

Mark held the school door open and they were hit by a wall of wind and noise.

'What is it, Big Guy?'

'Can I play on my DS when we get home?'

Mark braced himself for heading into the storm.

'Sure.'

They couldn't speak on the walk home, the wind whipping words away from their mouths when they tried. Nathan was having trouble even walking into the strongest gusts. This was ridiculous.

Mark looked at the sea. The whales were closer to the shore than before, bad news for them. The crowd had partly dispersed, no doubt fed up with the conditions out there.

Mark tapped Nathan on the shoulder and pointed at the whales. Nathan nodded and smiled. The whales were big news at school with the kids.

Mark and Nathan struggled round the bandstand and up Marlborough Street, past the detached houses to the flats at the top. Number 12, red door. Mark looked for Lauren's car, but it wasn't there. He got his keys out and opened the door. The silence in the stairwell was shocking after the roar of the wind.

3

Six o'clock and still no sign of her.

He'd lost count of the number of times he'd called her phone. Never anything. He'd phoned the Caledonia Dreaming office, no answer either on her direct line or at reception, but they were terrible at answering that thing. Then there was no point after 5 p.m. because they always closed on the dot.

He'd called the picture desk at the *Standard*, got another shutter-monkey to cover his shift. Fletcher didn't like it, but Mark had got some decent shots of the whale pod after all, so he was cut a little slack. Last thing he needed was to lose the gig at the paper, it was just about the only steady money he had coming in these days.

He got sausages, chips and beans on the table for him and Nathan and kept Lauren's warming in the oven. Your dinner is in the dog, and all that. She'd be in the door any minute. He would be cross at first that she hadn't called, that she'd left him in the lurch, but that would quickly dissipate into the usual comfortable family routine.

But something clawed at him. He flicked up the scan picture on his phone. He couldn't really make anything out, despite what the midwife and Lauren had said they could see. The baby supposedly had a spine and head already, fingers and toes, but all he could see was a swirl of white noise. It didn't seem real to him yet.

He couldn't help thinking about the last time. The depression after Nathan was born. The sense of alienation, something badly wrong. Then the disappearance. For ten days, right when he and Nathan had needed her most. The ten longest days in the history of the universe. Days spent at his wits' end, struggling with nappies, sterilisers, crying, sleepless nights, all piled on top of panic and worry, stress upon stress upon stress.

Then she reappeared, Mark furious and confused, mixed with relief that he didn't have to cope alone any more. Lauren was contrite but still desperate, almost suicidal at times, like a cornered beast. She never said where she'd been and Mark was too scared to ask. He didn't leave her alone with Nathan for two months after that. Horrible thoughts crept into his mind. Lauren went to counselling, struggled for months to bond with Nathan. Struggled for longer to reconnect with Mark. She refused drugs, distraught at the thought of her personality being altered by chemistry. It had all been such a battle, a sense of being battered by a storm, but they'd clung on and after eighteen months things had returned to something like an even keel.

That was all six years ago. But she was pregnant again, with a little girl this time. Maybe it was all coming back.

He tried to calm his breathing as he looked at the kitchen clock. The creeping second hand mocked him.

He turned to Nathan, who was stacking chips on his fork. Not exactly a healthy one today, but sod it, he couldn't think clearly enough to cook anything proper.

'So how was school today?'

'Fine.'

This conversation so familiar, like an anchor.

'What did you do?'

'Nothing.'

It was like a script, a game they played together.

'So you just sat there all day with Miss Kennedy doing nothing at all whatsoever?' Mark was hamming it up.

'Yes.' Nathan smiled, a smudge of bean sauce on his chin.

'OK, name me three things.'

Nathan did an exaggerated move, finger to cheek, head tilted, eyes upwards. Thinking boy.

'We did maths.'

'What kind of maths?'

'Doubling.'

'So what's double a million?'

That smile again. Just like Lauren's.

'That's easy,' Nathan said, rolling the words around and stretching them out. 'Two million.'

'What's double a billion?'

Nathan shook his head and sighed. Raised his eyebrows. 'Two billion.'

'OK, what's double infinity?'

'Infinity.' He wasn't to be fooled.

'Good stuff.'

Infinity was a thing at the moment, like Lego *Star Wars* and questions about death. The phases kids go through, like snakes shedding skins. *Super Mario Brothers* and *Ben 10* already far behind, *Bob the Builder* before that, *In the Night Garden* before that. Mark knew more about this little person than anyone would ever know about anyone else ever. But that would soon end, once the boy learned to hold secrets and keep stuff to himself.

He was in the top group for maths. He got that from Lauren who handled all the bills, she'd always been good with numbers. Top group for reading too, another thing he got from her. He struggled with his writing, though, which was probably Mark's legacy.

Not that it worked like that, of course. Mark could see from day one that Nathan was his own person with his own personality. Before they'd had him, Mark had presumed kids were empty vessels, ready to be filled in by the parents. How wrong could you be. Nature over nurture, easy. All you could do was try to stop them killing themselves and hope they didn't turn into crackheads or hookers. A lifetime of worry lay ahead. The joy of parenthood.

Nathan finished his sausages and Mark cleared the plates away.

'OK, second thing you did at school.'

'Comprehension.'

This was where they read a story then answered questions at the end, see if they'd understood it. Mark had read one that Nathan brought home, a thing about a mouse saving a lion from hunters after the lion had been nice to him. Pretty clunky, but a solid enough moral for P2s. Nathan seemed to like it anyway.

'Did you get all the answers?'

'It's easy, Daddy, the answers are always in the story.'

Mark smiled as he brought over a bowl of strawberries and yoghurt.

'All right, one last thing?'

'Gym.'

'Of course, Tuesday. What did you play?'

'Pirates.'

A fancy game of tig. Mark always worried about the physical side of things. Nathan was the youngest in the class, there were kids a full head taller than him, much bulkier too. But he was fast, always running everywhere. He just didn't care for the competitive element of sport. Like everything else, Mark wondered how that would translate into adulthood.

'Daddy, were you taking pictures of the whales earlier?'

'Yeah, I was.'

'Cool. Were any of them spyhopping?'

Mark smiled. 'How do you know about spyhopping?'

'Miss Kennedy told us all about it.'

'Yes, they were spyhopping, but I didn't get any pictures of it.'

'That's a shame. Will your pictures still be in the newspaper?'

'I think so. We'll see tomorrow.'

Nathan looked thoughtful for a moment. 'Miss Kennedy says the whales might die.'

'That could happen, but hopefully not. Everyone is trying to help them get back out to sea.'

'Why do they come in towards the beach?'

'No one really knows.'

'That's what Miss Kennedy says.'

Miss Kennedy was the voice of authority, apparently.

'Daddy, let's have a staring contest.'

This was the latest thing. Along with thumb wrestling and rock-paper-scissors, playing at seeing who would blink first. All the rage in the playground, it seemed.

Mark leaned in and stared at Nathan, whose eyes widened.

Mark began goofing around, making funny faces, and Nathan laughed, but he didn't blink, kept his gaze steady. The boy was good. Mark felt air against his eyeballs. The pressure built up until he felt himself flinch and blink. Damn it.

Nathan was triumphant. 'I win!'

'Well done, Big Guy.'

Mark remembered something. 'I've got a prize for you.'

'What?'

Mark reached into his pocket and took out the piece of sea glass.

Nathan was well chuffed. He took it in his hand and examined it like a diamond. Rubbed his fingers all over it. Something about that grainy surface was captivating. 'Cool.' He turned the piece upside down, so the fat end was at the top, and held it out to Mark. 'Look, it's a bit like a stormtrooper helmet.'

Mark laughed. It wasn't really, but good imagination. 'So it is.'

Nathan placed the piece down carefully on the table. 'I'll put it with the collection after tea.' He started into his strawberries and yoghurt.

Mark looked at the clock again. He'd distracted himself for all of five minutes talking to the boy, but now worry swamped back in.

If she just forgot it was her turn to pick up Nathan, she would've been home by now. Maybe she went shopping after work. That wasn't like her, and anyway, why would her phone be off? Out of juice? She was always forgetting to charge the bloody thing. She wouldn't have gone for a drink with anyone from Caledonia Dreaming after work either, she never did anything like that. And it was even less likely at the moment since she wasn't drinking and was so tired all the time. First trimester and all that. And sick too, not just in the mornings. Certain smells set her off – coffee, toothpaste, lilies. Maybe she'd gone to the doctor or hospital. But the surgery would be shut now, and it was crazy to phone the ERI when she'd only been gone for two hours. Wasn't it?

He kept coming back to the same thing. The time after Nathan was born. When she couldn't cope and had fallen off the earth for ten days, leaving him alone with the baby, having to explain to midwives and doctors and family and friends and then the police. But not really understanding it himself, just that she'd been down, had struggled to bond with the baby, struggled to cope.

'I'm finished,' Nathan said in a sing-song voice. 'Please can I come down?'

'Of course.'

'And please can I play on my DS again for a little bit?'

That was never usually allowed, not after tea, not on normal days. This wasn't a normal day and Mark needed time to think.

'Sure.'

Nathan made an exaggerated shocked face and Mark laughed.

'Weren't expecting that answer, were you?'

Nathan leapt towards him, all sharp elbows and frantic energy, and gave him a hug.

'Thank you, Daddy.'

Mark held on for a moment longer than usual, then let the boy go.

4

Still no sign of her by Nathan's bedtime. Mark peeled the boy away from his DS for the nightly routine, and he looked puzzled for a moment.

'Where did you say Mummy was?'

'I didn't.'

'Well, where is she?'

'She'll be home soon. It'll be after you're asleep, though.'

'Tell her to come in and give me a kiss.'

'I will, Big Guy, don't worry.'

Nathan tilted his head. 'I'm not worried.'

'Come on, let's get you into your jammies and get those teeth brushed.'

Nathan rough-housed his mouth with the brush. The first two of his milk teeth were loose, bottom row centre, and he was desperate to shake them out, cash in with the tooth fairy. Mark didn't like the deception of that, he disliked Christmas for the same reason. We spend our time warning kids to tell the truth, then feed them packs of lies whenever we get the chance. Lying to Nathan made him feel sick, even stupid little lies like the tooth fairy.

They both had a feel of the two teeth, shoogly but hanging on. Nathan pouted, flicking the teeth with his tongue.

'Maybe tomorrow,' Mark said.

He hustled Nathan into bed with a glass of warm milk. Nathan asked for *What Was I Scared Of?* for his bedtime story.

As usual for kids' books there was a moral shoehorned in there, but Dr Seuss handled it better than most, having written it before all that became so heavy-handed. The book was about someone scared of a spooky pair of empty pants. As in American pants, trousers. Mark had to explain the difference several times when they first read it. Tonight, when he got to the best bit, the lines where the little critter confessed to lying when he said he wasn't afraid, Mark felt a chill.

He left Nathan with the bedside light on and a *Clone Wars* comic open, and headed to the kitchen. Cracked a Beck's open and took a long slug. Half gone straight away with these tiny bottles. He remembered Lauren's dinner was in the oven. Opened the door and pulled it out. Shrivelled up and cold, fat congealed under the sausages. He tipped the contents into the bin, put the plate in the sink and went through to the living room.

Eight fifteen. She'd only technically been AWOL for five hours. He tried her mobile again. No answer. He flicked through the address book on his phone. Dreaded making calls to their friends, but he knew he would have to. Everyone knew about what happened last time. He would hear their thoughts down the line, their silent condemnation, in between the platitudes they churned out.

He went over to the desk, flipped the MacBook open and powered it up. Sat staring at the little logo. When the icons appeared he logged into her Gmail account. The password wasn't a secret, 'naphan1'. With a 'p' instead of a 't' after her account got hacked and spewed out weight-loss spam to all her contacts.

She had a few junk emails from Gap, Ikea, Amazon. An email from her work account, sent yesterday, probably just paperwork to do at home. It was blank with an attachment. He clicked on it. An Excel spreadsheet of numbers, the columns full of company acronyms. Nothing that made much sense. He closed it. No other emails. He checked her sent folder. Nothing today.

He went on to Facebook and checked her status. No activity since yesterday evening. Did the same with Twitter, but it was all quiet.

He blew out a sigh and sat back in the chair, then began phoning round the friends they still had in town. Not nearly as many as they'd had a few years ago. Kids got in the way of that, couples settling down, moving away, shifting themselves to places they could afford with gardens, nearer to grandparents, immersed in the middle of careers now.

Plus they'd never had that many friends anyway, no higher education background to gang them together with people. No real social networks except for the handful of folk they'd worked in bars with, but if ever there was a transient bunch, it was young pub staff. Mark hadn't kept in touch with anyone from school in Dundee, and Lauren couldn't wait to get away from the stuck-up bitches at the private Catholic school her mum and dad had paid fees for.

Of the few friends he called, no one had heard from her. No surprise. He tried to play it down, making the excuses he'd prepared in his head. No one bought it. He could tell from their voices they all thought she'd run off again, into the same dark place as before. He didn't blame them for thinking that.

That just left the hardest phone call of all. Ruth, Lauren's mum. He thought about it, tried to work it out in his head. He hadn't spoken to her or seen her in five years. Not since the big bust-up. It was technically against the law for him to phone her, with the restraining order. There was no time limit on that.

It had all come out when Lauren went to counselling and therapy. Not at the beginning, it took months for the therapist to dig down far enough. Searching for possible underlying reasons behind her postnatal depression. Eventually stumbling on Lauren's thing with her now-dead father. Not just the typical troubled father–daughter relationship. After some intense sessions, Lauren uncovered stuff she'd apparently suppressed her whole life, memories of her dad interfering with her, abusing her from when she was five to when she finally learned to say stop three years later.

Lauren never told her mum at the time, but looking back on it in the therapy sessions, she thought Ruth must have known. How could you not know something like that was going on under your own roof between the two people you were closest to in the whole world?

Lauren confronted her mum, who was horrified. She refused to believe such a thing could have happened. Couldn't believe that the man she'd loved her whole life was capable of something like that. She accused Lauren of making it up, finding an excuse for her own terrible behaviour in abandoning Nathan and Mark after the birth. A series of angry exchanges ended when Mark intervened. Ruth said some terrible things to the woman he loved, a woman struggling to get her sanity back together in the wake of it all, and Mark snapped.

He slapped Ruth in the face while they stood on her doorstep. Slapped her hard.

It ended the argument. And it ended Mark's relationship

with his mother-in-law. Ruth took out a restraining order against him. She and Lauren didn't communicate for almost a year. Finally a desire from Ruth to be a part of her only grandson's life brought some tentative conversations between mother and daughter, but it was never anything other than strained, and Mark wasn't allowed to be anywhere near Ruth when she came to visit. Not that she came often, maybe twice a year, things too awkward between her and Lauren.

And there was the added complication of Lauren's dad, the way William died. He just disappeared one day. Supposedly went out for a walk and didn't come home. It was a vanishing that was mirrored by his daughter two years later.

Only in William's case, there was nothing like depression that anyone knew of to explain it away. Although in retrospect, maybe he was haunted by his own demons. His body was found three months later nestled amongst the reeds at Portmore, his favourite fly-fishing haunt. The body was bloated and rotten, but there was no sign of violence. He had simply drowned. His car had been recovered long before that at Prestonfield Golf Club, which didn't make any sense. How did he get to Portmore? Why was he there? There was never any satisfactory answer and the police eventually closed the file.

All of which piled up on top of Mark now as he thought about phoning Ruth. But he had to know if Lauren had been in touch with her, so he pressed in her number.

'Hello, 449 4421.'

Such an old person thing to do, recite your number when you answer.

Mark rubbed his neck.

'Ruth.'

A long pause. 'You're not supposed to phone here, Mark.'

'I know.'

'I don't want to speak to you.'

Mark breathed in. 'Lauren's missing.'

Another pause. 'What do you mean, missing?'

'She didn't pick Nathan up from school today. I can't get hold of her.'

He heard her exhale down the line. 'My goodness, you had me worried for a second. That's only a few hours.'

'But it's not like her. She's not answering her phone.'

'I'm sure she's just out after work or something.'

'But why would her phone be off?'

'Maybe she wants to relax. Or maybe she can't get a signal.'

'Has she been in contact with you?'

'No.'

'I mean, at all in the last few weeks?'

'No, Mark. I haven't spoken to her since Nathan's birthday.'

'Are you sure?'

'Of course I'm sure, I know if I've talked to my own daughter or not.'

'OK.' Mark sucked in air. 'There's something else.'

A sigh down the line. 'What?'

'She's pregnant again.'

Crackle on the line, then quiet.

'Really,' Ruth said.

'Yes.'

Eventually Ruth spoke. 'I see.'

'She's about thirteen weeks gone now. We've had the first scan, everything seems normal.'

Mark thought back to the first time. He and Ruth had shared

something back then, the terror of Lauren's disappearance. For Ruth, it was compounded by the recent memory of William's death, the way that had happened. For Mark, it was compounded by the wide-eyed panic of fatherhood on his own. They had bonded after a fashion, Ruth helping out with the new baby when she could, the two of them forming an unlikely alliance.

Then they had thrown that away after Lauren's return. It was so easy to go from mutual support group to hated enemies, all it took was a simple truth being exposed.

'Don't worry.' Ruth didn't sound convinced by her own words. 'I'm sure she'll turn up soon.'

'What if she doesn't, Ruth?'

'We'll cross that bridge when we come to it.'

Mark thought about that 'we'. There hadn't been a 'we' between him and Ruth for a long time.

'Just let me know if she gets in touch,' he said.

'And you do likewise.'

He hung up. Rolled his neck and heard the cartilage crunch. His mouth felt dry. He went to the kitchen and opened another Beck's. Closed his eyes and held on to the sink with one hand as he glugged it down.

He tried Lauren's number again. Nothing.

He'd run out of options. He called Portobello Police Station. Got what sounded like a pubescent boy on the front desk who put him through to a young woman. DC Ferguson. She sounded the same age as Miss Kennedy, and that old line about coppers getting younger flitted through his mind.

'I'd like to report a missing person.'

'OK, sir, hang on till I find the form.'

He heard paper rustling. Took a deep breath.

'Right,' she said. 'Go ahead.'

'It's Lauren Bell, my wife.'

'And your name is . . .'

'Mark Douglas. She never took my name when we got married.'

Ferguson didn't care about that. 'Address, Mr Douglas?'

'Twelve Marlborough Street, flat three.'

'And how long has it been since you saw your wife?'

This was all too calm, too normal.

'She was supposed to pick our son up from school earlier.'

'Earlier today?'

'Yes, at quarter past three, but she never showed.'

'That's only six hours ago.'

'I know how long it's been.'

'How old is your wife, Mr Douglas?'

'Thirty-nine.'

'And I take it you've tried contacting her?'

'Of course I have, I'm not a fucking idiot.'

'OK, calm down, Mr Douglas, I appreciate this is a stressful situation for you.'

'Do you?'

'And you've phoned round friends, family, colleagues?'

'Obviously, or I wouldn't be calling the police.'

'The thing is, Mr Douglas, we can't log her as a missing person until she's been gone for a reasonable time.'

It sounded like she was reading from a script.

'What the hell is a reasonable time?' Mark said.

'That depends.'

'On what?'

'On whether your wife is in any of the risk categories.'

'What are the risk categories?'

'If she's suffering from mental or physical illness, depressed or suicidal, addicted to any substances or in any other way vulnerable.'

'Jesus, that's quite a list.'

'I realise this is hard, Mr Douglas.'

It was the second time she'd tried to be reassuring. He didn't feel reassured. She spoke again.

'Does your wife fall into any of these categories?'

Mark rubbed a knuckle in his eye and cricked his neck again. He thought about mentioning it, but that had all been six years ago. A lifetime, really, a different universe. She seemed fine recently, better than ever, and she was genuinely excited at the scan, eyes shining, full of life. He didn't have a reason to suspect her current mental state, no evidence that it was coming back. He couldn't get into this with the police, couldn't handle it right now.

'No,' he said.

'I see. Well, all I can do at the moment is give you a police incident report number. In the vast majority of these cases, the missing person turns up safe and sound in a very short space of time.'

'Is that it?'

'I would recommend that you phone the Accident and Emergency Department at the ERI just in case.'

'Jesus.'

'And I can give you the number for the Missing People twenty-four-hour helpline. They provide round-the-clock support for people in your situation.'

'My situation.'

'I'm sorry we can't do more at the moment, Mr Douglas. If your wife is still missing in, say, twenty-four or thirty-six hours' time, do please phone again and we can register this as an official missing persons case.'

'Is that the best you can do?'

'I'm sorry.'

She gave him the charity number and he scribbled it down on the back of a note from Nathan's school then hung up.

So much for the police.

He should've told them about the postnatal depression. He knew that, but he didn't want to go down that road. Not until he had to.

He went to the window and looked out. Almost dark now, just the outline of the disused church across the road, the Celtic cross on its roof stark against the violet fringe of sky behind.

He looked up the street, willing her car to come round the corner at the top, slowing at the speed bumps, searching for a parking space. Nothing. The wind was still gusting like crazy out there, making their old sash-and-case window rattle in its frame. He could feel the change of pressure in the room as the glass juddered.

He got the number for the hospital and called. Nothing. Unless she used another name, of course.

He got another beer from the fridge and came back.

He tried to think of this morning, to conjure up the last image of Lauren he had in his mind. It was the usual chaos of getting Nathan ready and out the door for school. Despite the fact the boy woke up at seven sharp every morning, they somehow always struggled to get out the door for half eight. He tried to think about how Lauren had been, if there was anything unusual. Did they kiss goodbye? Did she kiss Nathan? He couldn't remember. Just another day as a family.

Outside the window, a car trundled down the street. Wrong make and colour to be Lauren's.

Mark sighed and dragged his eyes away from the window, but he didn't shut the curtain. He looked around the room – brown leather sofas, shelves overstuffed with Lauren's thrillers and crime novels, cheap Ikea rug on the badly sanded floor. It was all familiar yet now somehow alien, replaced by exact replicas like on a film set.

Back out the window. No cars. The television aerials on the flats up the street were wobbling in the wind. The sound of each new gust outside made Mark tense his shoulders. He wondered if it was possible for their window to blow in.

He went through to his and Lauren's bedroom. The bed was still unmade from this morning. He went to her side of the bed and glided his hand over the sheet. No impression of her body, of course, that would be too dramatic, too symbolic. He bent down and put his nose to her pillow. Coconut and fruit, whatever that shampoo was she used. And something else lurking underneath, something undeniably her, a smell only he knew, a smell he had known for eighteen years.

They'd met in Smuggler's Tavern at the start of the nineties. It was a stupid name for a student pub, and neither of them were students, her pouring pints behind the bar, him drinking with a band he'd been photographing across the road at their Niddrie Street practice room.

He'd noticed her before, been in the pub a few times but never had the bottle to ask her out. Finally, after the band had bought him enough Aftershocks, he plucked up the courage.

She told him later that she never went out with punters, but had made an exception for him. Cute eyes. They both had shoulder-length hair back then, grunge was just catching on in Edinburgh, and the band Mark had been snapping earlier were apparently courting interest from a handful of labels, despite being a thin Pearl Jam rip-off.

Mark had come to Edinburgh after his dad died of a heart attack. His dad had raised him alone from the age of five, after his mum was diagnosed with aggressive Hodgkin's lymphoma. Mark was younger than Nathan was now when his mum died. He only had the tiniest fleeting memories of her, and he wasn't sure if they were even real, or if his mind had adapted them from old photographs or stories his dad told. Meeting a scary Santa in a shop while holding his mum's hand, sharing an ice cream on Broughty Ferry beach in a cold wind.

His dad had tried his best with Mark, but he wasn't a natural father, prone to anger easily, and Mark's teenage years saw the two of them drift into becoming more like flatmates than father and son, avoiding each other as much as possible.

When his dad died, Mark wasn't left with much, enough to buy his first decent camera and keep him afloat for a few months while he tried to make some money out of it.

He had no ties left in Dundee and wanted to see some action, so moved to Edinburgh, began touting for work with bands, artists, magazines and newspapers. Showed some talent and got work as a freelance, all the while doing his own more artistic photography on the side, landscapes and seascapes mostly. He even toyed with the idea of applying to study at the Art College at one point, but by then the work was coming in, and he'd got used to having drinking money in his pocket.

Lauren had similarly drifted. Maybe she saw a kindred spirit in him. Another only child, too. She was brought up in Upper Gray Street on the Southside, in the shadow of St Columba's, where she was dragged to mass every Sunday morning until she was old enough to refuse. Her parents had scraped together fees for her to go to St Margaret's Catholic girls' school, despite living in the catchment area for Gillespie's, one of the best comprehensives in the city. She hated it. The privileged posh girls looked down on her for only living in a flat rather than one of the bigger Southside houses. She left with no Highers despite being good at maths and English, and with no direction either, slipping from one side of the bar to the other, her tight body, beautiful smile and sharp brain perfect for working in the late-night haunts of Cowgate and Grassmarket.

After a first drunken date, and a fumbled snog up against the rough brickwork of the mortuary building at the bottom of Infirmary Street, they were inseparable, spending the days sleeping in Mark's tiny boxroom in Sciennes, the nights drinking, taking speed, smoking dope, shagging for hours back in that windowless room.

Thinking again about it now, it seemed to Mark like two other people in a parallel universe. Who were those lusting kids? How had the pair of them got through life, almost doubled in age, with their own kid now and all the stuff that went with that? And the problems. The depression, the disappearance, the therapy, the abuse, the bust-ups.

And now this.

He took a deep breath and stood up. Went to the wardrobe. More cheap Ikea, they were keeping that place in business. Went to his underwear drawer and dug both hands in. Pulled out his dad's old tobacco tin and opened it. A tiny knot of grass, left over from years ago, kept for old times' sake. He lifted it to his nose and inhaled. Then he closed the tin and replaced it. He rummaged right to the back of the drawer and pulled out a plain wooden box the size of a shoebox. Took his keys out his pocket. On the keyring was a small key that fitted the lock on the box. He unlocked it, opened it and lifted out a familiar object wrapped in a fawn shammy leather. Sat down on the bed and unwrapped it.

His grandfather's Browning hi-power 9 mm semi-automatic and a handful of bullets. A Second World War relic, passed down from his dad. Both father and grandfather were Dundee cops in their day, Mark had been the disappointment, not following in their footsteps. He checked the gun. Took the magazine out. It was empty. He ran through the trigger mechanism. Thought about squeezing the bullets into the magazine for a moment, but didn't. Then he replaced the empty magazine and sat holding the gun, flicking the safety on and off, feeling comfort in the easy slide of oiled metal.

Lauren hadn't taken it. That was a good thing. It was locked away for Nathan's sake. Mark wasn't sure why he kept it. That wasn't true, he knew exactly why he kept it, one of the few remaining links to his dad and grandad. No family left on his side, just him and Lauren starting again from scratch. There were only relics left from the past, the Browning and the tobacco tin linking him tenuously to what had gone before.

He and Lauren had argued about it. She didn't want a gun in the house, and he understood that. But he couldn't let go. Nathan didn't know about it, of course, and it was never loaded. And then there was the whole safety mechanism and the locked box, so it was as safe as it could be.

He almost threw it away last time she disappeared. She hadn't taken it with her then either, but when she returned, everything as fragile as rice paper, he'd hidden it amongst his camera equipment for a while, knowing she wouldn't think to look there. Terrible that he'd had those thoughts, that she might use it on herself. Or worse. Terrible but necessary thoughts.

'Daddy?'

Mark flinched. He had his back to the door, and he scrambled to wrap the Browning and bullets up in the shammy, then stuff them under the edge of the duvet.

'What is it, Big Guy?' He tried to keep his voice normal as he turned.

'I can't get back to sleep.'

Nathan's hair was tufty and his eyes half closed as he stood there in his *Clone Wars* jammies. Mark went to him and lifted him up, felt thin arms wrap around his neck.

'Come on, let's get you back to bed.'

'Is Mummy home yet?'

Mark felt his heart thumping against Nathan's chest, the two of them pressed so close together. Felt the boy's bony spine against his fingers.

'Not yet.'

They got to Nathan's room and Mark lowered him into bed, tucking him in.

'I had a bad dream,' Nathan said. 'Mummy was eaten by whales.'

'It's just a silly dream, Mummy's fine.'

'Can you stroke my head, Daddy?'

Mark kneeled down, smoothed out the stormtrooper bedspread. That iconic white mask staring up at him, hollow eyes.

'Of course, ten strokes.'

'Yeah, ten strokes.'

One of their infinite private confidences, tiny routines they'd worked out over six years of intimate living.

Mark stroked across Nathan's forehead and up the temple, through the hair behind the ear.

'One.'

Nathan was breathing deeply by four and asleep again by eight but Mark went to ten anyway. Then just stayed there on his knees, watching the boy breathe.

5

'Daddy, can I watch CITV?'

He felt the boy's hands shaking him and opened his eyes. He was on the sofa, a handful of empty beer bottles on the floor, kicked over. Still dressed from last night. The television was on, showing the Scottish news. Footage of the pilot whales this morning, very close to land, tumbling waves churning up against the shore, fins and snouts dipping in and out.

Mark straightened up. 'Sure.'

Nathan went for the remote as Mark headed out the door. *Almost Naked Animals* came on behind him.

Mark darted to the bedroom. Nothing had changed. No Lauren. Of course. He stumbled through the flat. Nothing. Checked the time. 7.04 a.m., Nathan up on the dot. Mark never understood how he did that. He dug the heels of his hands into his eye sockets then slapped himself on the cheek to wake up. He checked his phone. No messages, no missed calls. He tried her number, knowing full well he'd get nothing.

He went to the kitchen and stuck the kettle on, then the radio. Local news. The storm had blown trees and power lines down. The pod of whales still wasn't pushing out towards open sea, and the experts were worried. A local councillor had finally resigned after a corruption scandal. Crime figures had dropped thanks to more police on the streets, according to a government talking head. Mark thought about his conversation with DC Ferguson last night as he made himself a black coffee.

What now? Get Nathan to school, that was the first thing. Then head to the Caledonia Dreaming office, find out when they'd last seen her. Then what?

He stood there looking out the window at the trees in the back garden throwing themselves around in the wind, his mind churning. Eventually Nathan came through.

'Can I have breakfast now, Daddy?'

He snapped out of it. 'Of course, what do you want?'

'Cheerios. And Rice Krispies. Together.'

Mark made a face and smiled. 'Sit up at the table, then, I'll get it.'

He checked her Facebook and Twitter accounts again as he sorted breakfast. No activity. Logged on to her Gmail. Nothing new.

'Did Mummy not come home last night?' Nathan said between mouthfuls.

Mark had to make a decision. He hated lying, hated it, but sometimes it had to be done. What good would it do to tell the boy he had no idea where Mummy was? That she'd abandoned them when Nathan was a baby, and it looked like she'd done it again.

'She did come home, but she had to go to work again very early this morning.'

'Did she kiss me when she got in last night?'

'Of course.'

Another mouthful of combo cereal.

'Mummy works really hard, doesn't she?'

'Yeah, she does.'

'I don't mean that you don't work hard, Daddy.'

Mark liked that about Nathan, he was considerate of others' feelings. Good sign he wasn't going to grow up into a sociopath.

'I know, Big Guy.'

'Even though you don't work in an office like Mummy.'

'Just eat up, OK? Then we can start getting ready for school.'

*

The walk along the prom was a struggle, gusts knocking them sideways, sometimes stopping them in their tracks, Mark having to grip Nathan's hand.

It was bin day, and large green bins were scattered all across the prom, a few of them tipped over, seagulls hanging in the wind and eyeing the spilled contents.

Mark and Nathan walked along, making *Star Wars* blaster noises at the bins. Another of their games, pretending the bins were battle droids and blasting them to smithereens, Nathan totting up the points equivalent from his DS game. Mark had invented it one morning in P1 as a distraction technique when Nathan was being a pain about going to school.

'That gets us an extra life,' Nathan shouted over the wind, as they tag-teamed on the large communal bin at the bottom of Bath Street.

Mark looked out to sea and tried to spot the pilot whales. There was no boat on the water to guide his eye in the right direction, maybe it was too rough out there. And no one watching from the beach either. Perhaps the story had lost its appeal. He thought he saw a couple of fins, but the waves were so rough he couldn't be sure, and anyway, it was taking all his concentration to keep walking forward in this crazy weather. How long could it stay like this? Apparently it was the remains of an American hurricane. The joke doing the rounds was that the hurricane had been upgraded to a typical Scottish summer. Boom boom. But this was no joke, avoiding rolling bins and stopping your six-year-old from taking off.

The shoreline was littered with flotsam, broken trees, barrels, pieces of boat, swathes of bladderwrack. Mark had never seen so much crap washed up before.

'Keep shooting, Daddy,' Nathan shouted. 'You're six levels behind.'

Mark pointed his finger at a bin and did his best blaster. Nathan had got into *Star Wars* backwards, from the Lego *Star Wars* game on the DS to the Lego figures to the real films, the dreadful later ones first, of course. And don't even mention *The Clone Wars*. It seemed like there was a never-ending stream of cartoon DVDs to be bought and watched and dissected. Not that they made any bloody sense to Mark.

But the original films had their problems for a six-year-old too. All that stuff about Luke and Darth. How Darth is Luke's daddy, and he's evil, and they try to kill each other, then Darth saves Luke in the end. Take that, Oedipus. And don't even get started on Luke fancying his own sister.

It's amazing how your brain can soak up all this shit and birl through it in thirty seconds flat, thought Mark. Anything to stop worrying about Lauren for a moment.

They arrived at the playground, full of kids trying not to get lifted off their feet.

Mark knelt down. 'Kiss.'

35

He felt Nathan's dry lips against his. Forgot to put Vaseline on them, they'd be cracked by home time. He did the hair tousle thing. He could still get away with that. Pretty soon Nathan would be rejecting all physical contact, in that way older kids do to assert their independence. Mark hugged the boy and felt him wriggling to get free. He handed over the obligatory *Clone Wars* lunchbox, straightened up and stepped back.

Nathan shuffled over to where the boys from his class were huddled. No interaction between the sexes – had it been like that when Mark was a kid? He couldn't remember. Nathan barely even seemed to realise girls existed. Another thing that would change soon enough.

Nathan was chatting to Keiran, a full year older than him and much taller, a good kid though. The bell went, barely audible over the whipping wind, and there was some argy-bargy between Nathan and one of the bampots, Lee, as they jostled to get in line. Nathan never normally got involved in all that aggressive boy shit, another thing Mark loved about him. But he could be provoked like anyone.

Back when they started P2, the oneupmanship was much worse, some of the boys seriously violent with real behaviour problems, but Miss Kennedy seemed to have sorted all that out.

She appeared at the classroom door, hair swirling into her mouth as she ushered the kids in. Nathan waved as he jogged in, Mark waving back in exaggerated fashion.

As soon as Nathan was inside the door, Mark turned and strode away.

On the walk back along the prom, he looked out for the whales again. Couldn't see anything in the churning wash.

He thought about how many times he'd walked up and down this bloody promenade. Thousands. He knew every inch of it, from pounding along pushing Nathan in his buggy when he wouldn't sleep, which was all the time for the first few months. Those terrifying days alone with the boy, wondering if Lauren was dead, where she was, what had happened, walking mile upon mile to get Nathan to go over to sleep, scared to return to the silence of the flat, knowing the baby would start crying again as soon as the motion of the buggy stopped, walking himself into a trance, a fretful, crushing mess of fear, anger and panic.

He reached the bottom of Marlborough Street and turned to the sea. The vastness of it normally helped Mark get perspective on the stupid little worries of everyday life. Not today.

6

As he swung the Peugeot into Circus Place, Mark got a familiar feeling that he was lowering the tone of the neighbourhood. He'd been this way plenty of times to pick Lauren up for lunch or go shopping after work, and he could never shake off the idea that his sort wasn't supposed to sully the regimented Georgian streets around here.

He parked outside the Caledonia Dreaming office and shuffled up the steps, eyeing the luxurious sculpted shrubbery that flanked the heavy front door. He slunk through the glass and brass vestibule, scuffing over the marble floor, then he was into the reception area.

They were clearly doing all right for themselves. Caledonia Dreaming was a high-end estate agency that specialised in snapping up rural plots of land, dilapidated mansions, top-of-the-range city properties and even country estates, then flogging them on at a profit. They seemed to have been completely bulletproof during the recent recession, the richest of the rich unaffected by the slump and as keen as ever to buy up Scottish real estate and the history that went with it. In fact, the company had positively blossomed in the last few years, as the old moneyed gentry of the upper classes struggled to hold on to their legacy, and all the usual oligarchs and bankers bought up property, eager to invest in their own Highland havens.

Mark didn't recognise the receptionist, but he recognised the type – posh Edinburgh, impeccably groomed, barely out of her teens but already assured and entitled. This was a classy little stepping-stone gap-year job on the way to investment analyst or rich housewife depending how the cards fell.

She glanced at him, looked him up and down, then returned her gaze to a sleek Mac on the huge mahogany desk. Obviously realised he wasn't rich enough to bother with. Tap, tap, tap. Making him wait.

'Can I help you?' she said.

'I'm Mark, Lauren Bell's husband?'

Blank look.

'Lauren? Chief sales agent?' Mark couldn't help putting inverted commas round the job title with his voice, as Lauren had done with her more lowly 'executive sales agent' for the first few months after she joined the company.

'Oh, Miss Bell, I didn't realise she was married.'

'Well, she is. To me.'

Those eyes again. She was thinking how Mark was punching well above his weight with Lauren. He was used to seeing that in people's faces.

'Miss Bell isn't in yet this morning.'

'I need to know when she was last in the office.'

The girl frowned. 'Why do you need to know that?'

'What?'

'It's a strange thing to be asking about your wife, that's all.'

'I just need to know.'

'Can I see some ID?'

'What?'

The girl looked at her manicured nails then back up. 'You could be anyone. A stalker.'

'For Christ's sake.' Mark dug in his pocket, pulled out his driver's licence and handed it over.

'This says "Mark Douglas".'

'Lauren never took my name. Look, I don't have time for this.'

'I'm sorry.' The girl handed back the licence. 'We can't give that sort of information to just anyone.'

'Don't be bloody ridiculous.' Mark puffed his cheeks and blew out. 'OK, I need to see Gavin Taylor, then.'

'I'm sorry, Mr Taylor is in meetings all morning. If you'd like to . . .'

Mark turned. 'Never mind, I'll go and find him.'

He strode through a set of glass doors, further into the building.

The girl called after him but he was gone, down the corridor, all landscape paintings and expensive spotlights. Smell of new carpet. He scanned the names on the doors. Of course, Taylor's was the biggest, a solid brass nameplate with 'Managing Director' written underneath.

Mark knocked and waited. The receptionist would've phoned ahead.

'Come in.'

Gavin Taylor was putting the phone down as Mark came in. He stuck on a smile and stepped out from behind his desk.

'Mark, how's it going?'

He held out a meaty hand. Mark shook it, feeling the bones ripple in his knuckles.

Gavin was a classic Scottish rugby type, private Edinburgh

school, prop-forward physique wrestled into an Ede & Ravenscroft suit. He was shorter than Mark but probably weighed seventy pounds more, all of which was muscle. Army-buzz hair, plummy vowels, he was charming with the underlying threat that his physical presence gave him.

Mark had known Gavin for over ten years, but never closely, and he'd never liked him. Gavin and his Edinburgh Uni rugger-bugger chums used to drink in the Last Drop during a spell when Lauren worked there, loud, braying guys with a gang mentality and an air of superiority. He flirted with Lauren off and on, advances she gently but firmly rebuffed, pointing out that she already had a boyfriend. Gavin never said as much, but he clearly couldn't believe Lauren would choose Mark over him.

In time, he'd backed off on the flirting, but had remained friendly with Lauren, Mark just having to put up with it. Then, a while after he had set up his own property company with some help from his rich dad, he offered Lauren a job in sales.

Lauren and Mark discussed it. He wasn't keen on her working with this guy, but he trusted her. They'd been together as a couple for years at that point, and although they hadn't said as much, it was clear they both felt that this was it for the rest of their lives. No need for words, they both just knew.

Lauren wasn't mad keen on sales either, she didn't have any experience. But Gavin pointed out that she was good with people and good with numbers, and that was just about all you needed. Plus he offered her twice as much money as she was scraping together as a barmaid. And you couldn't work in pubs all your life. With a decent, steady income, they could think about putting a deposit down on a place of their own, maybe even afford to go on holiday.

That was all eight years ago. A change in the direction of their lives, but a good one, one that had paid off. Gavin had got married to a suitable member of the Edinburgh elite, and the flirting of the Last Drop was consigned to history.

Lauren had turned out to be a good saleswoman, the right mix of outgoing charm and hard-nosed business sense. Her salary had increased, and she began snaring bonuses when times were good. She rose up quickly to the point where she was the top agent, and Gavin offered her a junior partnership in the firm. She and Mark had talked about the offer, it was a big step. She had to take out a hefty business loan to buy in, but the rewards were potentially much bigger. As were the risks, of course, if the company got into trouble. But there had been no sign of that so far. Mind you, there was precious little sign of rewards for Lauren either, with the loan repayments cancelling out her share of the profits. But it was a long-term plan that would hopefully come good eventually.

The whole business about Lauren's depression after Nathan was born was kept a secret from Gavin, no need to introduce any element of doubt about her state of mind with her senior partner and company MD. Plus her disappearance, return and recovery all occurred during her maternity leave anyway.

Since Nathan was born, Mark had only met Gavin a handful of times at Caledonia Dreaming events, wine and canapé affairs in swanky George Street venues, the company once hiring out the whole of Tigerlily for a banquet. Mark always felt out of place at those things, but played the game for Lauren's sake, glad-handing and smiling. The free champagne helped.

'If you're looking for Lauren, I don't think she's in yet,' Gavin said.

'I need to know when she was last in the office.'

'Is something wrong?'

'I just need to know.'

'Is there some kind of trouble at home?'

Mark shook his head. 'That's not what this is about.'

Gavin put a hand lightly on Mark's shoulder. A confident movement. 'Because I don't want to get in the middle of a domestic, if that's what's going on.'

'It's not that.' Mark swithered, looked around the office. Minimalist, expensive. Oak shelving and furniture, marble fireplace, swirling cornicing. Trees shuddered and shook outside the big bay window.

He turned to Gavin. 'She never came home last night.'

Gavin removed his hand. 'What?'

'She didn't pick Nathan up from school. Didn't come home. I haven't been able to get in contact with her.'

Gavin put on a concerned face. 'Have you called the police?'

'Of course, last night, but they said they can't do anything until she's been missing for longer.'

'That's ridiculous.'

'It's the rules.'

Gavin tugged at his cuffs. 'Well, she seemed fine in the office yesterday.'

'So she was at work?'

'Yes, we had a quick meeting in the morning, then she left at lunchtime.'

'She didn't come back?'

'Took a half day.'

'She never mentioned it to me.'

Gavin shrugged. 'Said she had some stuff to do.'

'When exactly did you last see her?'

Gavin rubbed his earlobe. 'Just before twelve. Like I said, we had a meeting.'

'What about?'

'Just a property we're in negotiation about.'

'Which property?'

Gavin frowned. 'An estate outside Longniddry.'

'Would she have gone out there?'

A shake of the head. 'We don't own it yet. Anyway, she was off work in the afternoon, I told you.'

Mark breathed out heavily, unclenched his fists. 'I know, I'm sorry. I'm just worried.'

'I can imagine.' Gavin's hand went back on to Mark's shoulder, it was meant to be comforting.

'I don't know what to do.' Mark rubbed at his forehead.

'I'm sure she's fine. Maybe she just needs a bit of space.'

Mark looked at Gavin. He was rubbing his earlobe again.

'Why would you say that? Space from what? Me?'

'Take it easy. I didn't mean anything.' Gavin began ushering Mark towards the door. 'Look, why not go home and wait for her. I'm sure she'll turn up soon enough. If she gets in contact with the office, I'll have her call you straight away. OK?'

Mark wanted to do something, say something. He shrugged off Gavin's hand.

'I have to do more than just sit at home,' he said. 'She's fuck-ing missing, don't you understand? I have no idea where my wife is.'

'Of course I understand. I would feel exactly the same in

your position. I would be beside myself if Sarah-Jane disappeared. But the best thing you can do is wait for Lauren to get in contact, and keep in touch with the police.'

Gavin opened the office door. 'I'm sure it'll all be fine. Try not to worry.'

'I'm fed up of people telling me that.'

The door closed and Mark stood there rubbing his face with his hands.

He turned and walked down the corridor. Took a left turn to Lauren's office. Stood outside her door and looked at the nameplate. Miss Lauren Bell. Chief Sales Agent. It was mostly out of sheer laziness that she had never taken his name. And she never corrected the 'Miss' at work. Turned out to be quite an advantage in business deals with middle-aged men, a bit of flirting, the illusion of availability. Mark resented the implications of that, how could he not. But it wasn't a big deal because he trusted her.

He turned the handle and was surprised to find the door open. He went inside. It was smaller than Gavin's office, no great view out the window, cheaper fixtures and fittings, no fireplace. A seascape on one wall and a shelf of folders and binders on the other.

He walked to her desk. Neat, organised. Two small piles of paperwork, contracts or similar. A Mac, switched off. A notepad with scribbles on it next to the phone. A picture of her, Mark and Nathan taken on the beach at Brodick in Arran, their first holiday together as a family. Nathan was clutching a toy police van in his hand. He had carried that with him the whole holiday. Lauren looking tired but contented. Two old golfers were on the course behind them, one in mid-swing. A moment captured in time forever.

He tried the desk drawer. Another notepad, Post-Its, a stapler, some business cards, a hole-punch, another neat pile of paperwork. Nothing unusual.

He shut the drawer and leaned on the desk with his knuckles, concentrating on breathing in and out. Looked around the office again then left, closing the door softly behind him.

As he passed through reception, the posh girl gave him daggers. There was a man waiting on a sofa, another of Edinburgh's privileged in a pinstripe suit, handkerchief in the breast pocket, handsome, carefully trimmed wavy hair. He was ages with Mark but looked younger. Mark was sick of all these rich, beautiful people already. The man watched blankly as Mark gave a sarcastic smile to the receptionist and left. He could feel her stare on him as he stumbled out the door.

7

From outside, Portobello Police Station was a beautiful old building, all turrets and crenellations. Inside it was a dump – jaundiced striplights, fag-burned furniture, smell of piss.

Mark approached the front desk, where a spotty kid in uniform was doodling.

'Is DC Ferguson about?'

The kid looked startled at being spoken to. 'I'll see if she's available, sir. What's your name?'

'Mark Douglas.'

'And will she know what it's regarding?'

'I spoke to her last night about a missing person.'

'Take a seat, please.'

The kid picked up the phone. Mark examined the stains on the seats and stayed standing. He shifted his weight from one leg to the other and stared blankly at crime-prevention posters. No knives, better lives. Cut out hate crime. Boozed up, squared up, locked up.

'Mr Douglas?'

He turned. DC Ferguson was short and slim, shoulder-length brown hair in an expensive cut, thin white blouse and black skirt. Her make-up was pristine and she had a smattering of freckles across her nose. She looked even younger than she sounded on the phone, and had an enthusiastic smile.

'Hi, we spoke last night,' Mark said.

'I remember. Your wife. Has she been in contact?'

'No, that's why I'm here.'

'Do you have some new information?'

'I've just been up at her work. She left at lunchtime yesterday, took a half day. I didn't know anything about that.'

Ferguson raised her eyebrows. 'Well, that's not necessarily bad news, Mr Douglas. It could mean there was an element of premeditation about her disappearance. She might've been planning something.'

'If Taylor was telling the truth.'

'Taylor?'

'Lauren's boss.'

'Wait.' Ferguson went to the spotty kid at the desk and borrowed his pad and pen. 'Where does your wife work?'

'Caledonia Dreaming. It's a property place in the New Town.'

'And what does she do there?'

'She's chief sales agent. Basically negotiates deals. She's a junior partner in the company.'

'And this Mr Taylor?'

'He's managing director.'

'And you just spoke to him?'

'Yeah, he said he had a meeting with Lauren yesterday morning, then she left at lunchtime. But . . .'

Ferguson frowned. 'What?'

Mark tried to remember the conversation. 'What if he's lying?'

'Do you have any reason to think he might be?'

Mark shook his head. 'Not really. I don't know. Just a feeling.'

'Well, we can speak to Mr Taylor in good time, if we need to.

I'm sure it won't come to that, your wife will probably turn up very soon.'

Mark scratched at his scalp. 'People keep telling me that, it really doesn't help.'

Ferguson looked at her watch, then back towards the desk.

'OK, look, I can see you're upset. I think we can turn this into an official missing person report, if you want.'

'Yes, definitely.'

'We'll need to get lots of details from you.'

'Like what?'

'A list of friends and family, places your wife might frequent, financial details, car registration, phone number, email accounts, everything.'

'Not a problem.'

'And we'll need a couple of recent photographs and a DNA sample.'

'A sample?'

'Her toothbrush or hairbrush maybe.'

'Oh. OK.'

'And we need consent to search your home.'

'What?'

'Standard procedure.'

Mark drew his fingers like a pincer across his eyes. 'Sure. Fine.'

He felt a hand on his arm. Everyone was always trying to comfort him. He didn't feel comforted.

'Look,' Ferguson said. 'Why don't we go there first? I'm sure there's nothing to worry about. For all you know, she might be at home wondering where you are.'

Mark shook his head. He knew there wasn't a hope in hell that was true.

8

It was intrusive, having a stranger rummaging through their stuff. Abusive, somehow. Lauren wouldn't like it.

They rarely had people round to the flat these days. Since Nathan was born and everything that Lauren went through afterwards, the opportunities for socialising had withered. Friends moved away, all of them focusing on their own lives, setting up their little shells, safe from the outside world.

And now here was a police officer, a woman barely out of her teens, going from room to room. Mark saw the place through her eyes, the worn patches on the hall carpet, the dust bunnies under Nathan's bed, the burnt food stains on the old cooker. It was like putting their whole lives on display, a personal museum exhibition.

Ferguson didn't appear to know what she was doing. Picking things up, putting them back again. She stopped at some pictures stuck to the fridge by magnets, flipped over a postcard.

This was useless. Shouldn't they be out looking for Lauren?

Ferguson sauntered through the flat, Mark trailing behind. She went into the couple's bedroom. Opened and shut the bedside drawers. Rennies and paracetamol on his side. A couple of books on Lauren's, Pelecanos and Leonard. He could never be bothered to read. Easier to watch the films when they came out.

Ferguson went to the wardrobe. Mark remembered the

Browning and the old grass tin, felt a weight descend on him, his eyelids suddenly heavy. No licence, never any licence, the pistol liberated after the war by his grandad. Not handed in after Dunblane either. Stupid, but there you are.

He didn't want the gun to become a sideshow, a distraction from the search for Lauren.

Ferguson was flicking through Lauren's blouses, skirts and dresses.

Mark approached and stood close to her.

'I don't think there are any clothes missing, if that's what you're looking for.'

She turned to him. 'Just background, really, Mr Douglas.'

'Call me Mark.' He edged towards the drawers. 'Did you say something about needing financial statements?'

'Please. Any bank accounts, savings plans, mortgage, life assurance, all that.'

Mark hesitated. 'OK, I'll go and dig that stuff out. Do you want a coffee? You can wait in the living room if you like.'

'Coffee would be great.'

Ferguson opened Lauren's underwear drawer. Shuffled some panties around at the front. Closed it. Then she opened his drawer. Did the same. Pushed it closed.

She missed it.

'Are you OK, Mr Douglas?'

Mark was standing holding the wardrobe door, eyes closed. 'Fine.'

'I realise how stressful this is for you, but the police are here to help.'

'I know.'

She closed the wardrobe doors, Mark lowering his hand.

'Now, let's get that coffee and go through the paperwork, shall we?'

She led him out of the room.

Mark switched the kettle on and went rooting for files. Flicked through and found all the stuff. Brought it back and handed it over. Gave Ferguson a description of Lauren's car, number plate, her mobile number, then went and got her toothbrush.

'This seems weird,' he said, handing it over.

Ferguson placed it in a small, see-through zip-lock bag, then into a pocket.

'I know it does, but I can assure you it's entirely routine.'

They got their coffees and moved to the tiny office corner of the living room, really just a desk and a laptop. Mark fired up the MacBook.

'I don't have any recent pictures printed out, but I could email a couple to you.'

'That's fine.'

Ferguson handed over a card with her email address and phone number on it. DETECTIVE CONSTABLE TRACEY FERGUSON. Tracey with an 'e'.

Mark clicked down through the picture folder on the desktop. Ferguson picked two and he emailed them to her address.

'What about your wife's email?' she said.

'She has a Gmail account. I've already checked it, we know each other's passwords. There's nothing in there that I could see.'

'I'd like the username and password all the same, so we can check it in more detail later.'

He wrote it down for her. Every bit of information he handed over seemed to make this more real, more concrete. She was really missing. Gone again.

His pulse became loud, thudding in his ears. His lungs seemed to collapse, and he struggled to take shallow breaths. His hands began to shake. He put the pen down and gripped the edge of the desk to steady himself. His vision seemed to roll on its axis.

'Mark?'

He felt Ferguson's hand on his, a tiny, bony thing. Not like Lauren's hands at all. His fingers trembled against the scratchy wood of the desk. The shaking spread up his arms to his body, and he raised a hand to his face. Tears fell on to the desk and he wiped his eyes, trying to regain control.

'It's OK,' Ferguson said. 'We'll find her.'

He tried to fill his lungs, then he pulled his hand out from under hers and sat back, blinking away tears.

'I didn't tell you last night.'

'What?' She was perched on the edge of the desk, close to him. He could smell lemony perfume.

Mark shook his head. 'Lauren has suffered from depression in the past. Postnatal, after Nathan was born. She disappeared for days.'

'I see. Do you know where she went?'

Mark shook his head. 'She never said. I was too afraid to ask. I wanted to know, but at the same time I didn't want to scare her away again. It was horrible. I think she was in a hotel some-where, maybe still in Edinburgh, I don't know.'

'What about her work?'

Mark's breathing calmed, his head cleared a little.

'What about it?'

'You said earlier about her boss, Mr Taylor.'

'Gavin, yeah.'

'You think he was hiding something?'

'I don't know.'

Ferguson straightened up, shifted her weight to create distance between them.

'This isn't an easy thing to ask.'

He rubbed his eyes. 'I know what you're going to say.'

'Do you think Lauren might be having an affair?'

'No.'

'Are you sure?'

He rubbed at his hair. 'Of course I'm not fucking sure.' His voice was louder than he expected. 'I have no clue any more about what she might've been doing or thinking, clearly. She's gone, isn't she?'

'OK, take it easy.'

'I don't want to take it easy, I want to find my wife.'

'Look, I'll pay a visit to the Caledonia Dreaming office, talk to Mr Taylor. I need to get access to her work email and files anyway.'

'I can't believe I need to think about this,' Mark said.

'I'm sorry.'

'Now you've got me worrying that Lauren was being unfaithful.'

'I have to ask these things.'

'Any other ideas you want to poison my mind with?'

'There is something else I need to ask.'

'Jesus.'

'Have you ever given your wife reason to leave?'

Mark rolled his neck and stood up so he was standing over her.

'Like what? Sleeping around? Hitting her?'

She held out a placatory hand. 'I have to ask.'

He held one fist in the other, as if clutching an injured bird. 'Nothing like that. We're happy together.'

She stared at him for a moment and he looked away, his gaze falling on the laptop screensaver, a picture of Lauren, Nathan and him taken at East Links Family Park, all smiling. He remembered it was a bitterly cold day, they only spent a few minutes feeding the animals then ducked into the cafe for hot chocolates. Ordinary family stuff. Everything called into question now.

Ferguson was shuffling the paperwork against the desk.

'I'll have all this copied and get it back to you. And I'll pay a visit to Caledonia Dreaming. I'll be in touch soon.'

Mark turned to her. He didn't like the look in her eyes.

'What am I supposed to do in the meantime?' he said.

'Just try to stay calm.'

Mark wished people would stop telling him that.

9

Upper Gray Street was a respectable and quiet line of terraced houses, only broken up by the modest church halfway down. Many of the houses had been split into lowers and uppers, and most of the lofts had been converted.

Bushes in the tiny front gardens shivered in the wind as Mark tried to find a parking space. He eventually got one near the top, a permit holders' place, but sod it, he would take his chances.

He got out and walked to number 22. The door had 'Bell' on the nameplate.

He hadn't set eyes on this front door in five years, ever since he'd stood on the step and assaulted his mother-in-law. He was ashamed about that now, that slip, a permanent stain on his life. He'd let his anger get the better of him. He worried at the time about it, whether he was destined to repeat his father's short temper, flying off the handle at the smallest thing. His dad hardly ever hit Mark as a kid, but he was quick to bawl him out at every opportunity, so that Mark soon learned to tune it out, become immune, which only led to more impotent rage from his dad.

But the incident with Ruth hadn't been the start of anything as far as he could tell. Mark got angry, sure, who didn't, but so far he'd managed to keep a lid on it. He tried especially hard around Nathan, despite the boy infuriating him at times with the standard kid stuff, the pushing of boundaries, the testing of limits, how far could he go before Mark or Lauren would flip out and the boy gained control. It was all normal family dynamics, but it was new to Mark and Lauren, this sudden subconscious battle for power within their home.

Mark pressed the doorbell. Heard a familiar two-tone chime he hadn't heard in years. Waited. Nothing. He pressed it again. No answer.

He stepped back a few paces and looked at the house.

Ruth had the ground-floor flat, the double upper owned by an old spinster Mark couldn't remember the name of now. The whole street was populated by over-sixties, folk who had bought when property was cheap in Edinburgh, way back in the mists of time. The houses were small and old but they were impeccably laid out, the kind of homes that were out of the reach of most young families. That and the tiny gardens made them a dim prospect for anyone with kids, with the result that hardly any new blood had entered the street in twenty years.

Mark remembered the last time he was here. Like a kind of summit meeting. Lauren, Ruth and him around the kitchen table, Nathan asleep in his buggy parked in the hall. Lauren telling Ruth what William had done all those years ago to their only daughter. How ashamed Lauren had felt, guilty, how she'd buried it so deep.

And Ruth refusing to believe. Getting angry, furious at her daughter, accusing her of slander, of avoiding taking responsibility for her own actions. The noise of their shouts woke Nathan in the hallway, who began crying.

Mark became more irate at Ruth's attitude to Lauren, the

daughter she'd given birth to and allowed to be abused under this very roof.

Ruth had bustled them all down the hall and out the door, then gave a parting shot to the effect that if something had gone on between William and Lauren, which she still denied, then it must've been because Lauren had brought it on herself.

The idiocy of that, the venom in it, made Mark's vision go blurry. The next thing he knew he'd struck her, hard, and she was staring at him with wet eyes, holding her cheek, a trickle of blood at her lip.

He heard something now above the wind whipping down the street. He looked to his right and saw three elderly women struggling up the hill. Ruth and two others. One popped into a house a few doors down with a short wave.

Then Ruth glanced up and saw him. Her pace slowed but she kept walking. The woman with her looked at Mark, then Ruth, then put out a supportive hand to her elbow. The women exchanged a few words, then the one Mark didn't know went into the house next to Ruth's.

Ruth stopped at her gate, opened it and came into the garden.

'What are you doing here?'

'I need to speak to you.'

'You're not allowed to be here.'

'I know, Ruth. But Lauren's still missing. I don't know what to do.'

Ruth looked at him for a long time, then went into her purse and took out her house key. She walked past him, keeping her eyes straight ahead. She unlocked her front door then turned to him. 'You'd better come in.'

10

The house hadn't changed at all. Dark wood, patterned wallpaper, thick carpets. Gloomy light seeping in through the windows.

Ruth walked to the kitchen without speaking to Mark. He shut the front door and followed her.

In the kitchen she lifted the kettle to the tap, filled it, then put it on. Got a teapot and mugs down from a cupboard. A routine she'd gone through for God knows how many years.

Mark watched her as she moved. She was tall like Lauren, but with a slight stoop now. Her wavy red hair was tied back in a loose ponytail in a style much younger than her years, a style Lauren used as well. Her body had thickened with age but still had a curve to it, and she wore a neat purple blouse and skirt, a green cardigan clutched round her.

When the tea was ready she lifted it over to the table and nodded for him to sit.

He took a chair opposite and looked at her. The same green eyes as Lauren and Nathan, the same strong jaw. He had a fleeting glimpse of the generations spiralling all the way back through time, just a flash of history.

'I'm sorry,' he said.

'What for?'

'Hitting you. Back then. I shouldn't have done that.'

'No, you shouldn't.' She placed a mug of tea in front of him, then put her hands around her own mug. 'You know, in my day, hitting a woman was considered a terrible thing.'

Mark sipped his tea. Still too hot. 'Hitting anyone is a terrible thing.'

'So you haven't heard from Lauren?' Ruth's face softened, her eyes worried.

'No.'

'Have you called the police?'

Mark nodded. 'I phoned last night, they made it an official missing person case this morning. I had an officer searching the flat earlier.'

'Searching the flat?'

'It's routine.'

Ruth nodded. 'Yes, I think I recall that from when William went missing.'

'They'll probably be in touch with you soon.'

'I wish I had something to tell them.'

'To be honest, I don't think they're that bothered about finding her yet. They think she just wandered off for a bit of peace and quiet or something.'

'Did you tell them about what happened after Nathan was born?'

Mark nodded.

Ruth looked at him. 'You think it's happening again? With her being pregnant?'

Mark ran a hand through his hair. 'I don't know. I just need to talk to someone about it. No one else knows her like you do.'

'I probably don't know Lauren as well as you think. It's not as if I've seen her much since Nathan was born.'

What she meant was she hadn't seen her much since Lauren had accused her own father of child abuse.

'I realise that it can't have been easy for you,' Mark said.

'What do you mean?'

'What Lauren said. About William.'

Ruth gripped her mug. She looked down at the swirling tea, thin slivers of steam drifting up from the surface. She turned and looked out the window, avoiding his gaze.

'Try to think how you would feel,' she said. 'How Lauren would feel if Nathan said that you had been . . .'

Mark felt a knot in his stomach. 'I know. It's difficult. But I don't think she made it up, Ruth.'

Ruth looked back at her tea. Took a deep breath.

'I don't think so either.' She looked up at Mark. 'You can't imagine what it's been like. Lauren and I have talked about it a little. I was so angry at first. What she said turned my whole marriage, my whole life, into a lie. Or worse. To begin with Lauren thought I was complicit, that I knew about it and didn't do anything.'

Her eyes were wet but she didn't look away.

'Trust me, Mark, if I had known . . . Mary Mother of God help me, I don't know what I would've done to William if I had known at the time. But I didn't. We went on living as a married couple for twenty-five more years. A quarter of a century of lies. My husband, the man I trusted with my life, the man I loved. He had the most filthy, disgusting secret you could imagine and I, like a naïve idiot, shared a bed with him, went on holiday with him, fretted about him when he went missing, cried my eyes out over him when they found him, then again when we buried him.'

She used the back of her hand to wipe the tears running down her cheeks. She sniffed.

61

'I feel so ashamed, Mark.'

'You have nothing to feel ashamed about.'

'Yes I do. Ashamed and guilty. Lauren is my daughter, I gave birth to her, I breastfed her and changed her nappies and rocked her to sleep. It was my job to take care of her, to make sure nothing bad ever happened. And I failed. I let the worst possible thing happen to her. I let a monster scare her and hurt her in our home and I defended his memory when she first accused him of it. I'm just as much of a monster as he was.'

Mark reached out a hand and placed it on Ruth's. Felt the loose skin across her knuckles.

'You're not a monster. There was nothing you could do. You didn't know.'

'I should've noticed. I should've seen something, should've suspected. I lie awake at night thinking about all the things I could've done differently, all the times William and Lauren were alone together. What was I doing? What was I thinking? What was he doing to her?'

More tears. She pulled her hand out from under his and wiped at her face again.

'Why couldn't she tell me? I'm her mother, for God's sake. Things can never be the same between us, not after everything that's happened.' She sighed. 'And now she's missing again.'

She dissolved into tears.

Mark reached for her hand again but she pulled away, tried to straighten herself out. She tugged a tissue from her cardigan sleeve and dabbed at her eyes. Sniffed a few times then blew her nose.

'Did you know that three hundred thousand people go missing in Britain every year?' she said.

'What?'

She took a sip of tea. 'They told me when William vanished.'

'Who did?'

'Missing People. Have you called them yet?'

Mark shook his head.

'About half of those people turn up safe and sound.'

'Which means that half don't,' Mark said.

'Yes.'

'Do you think William killed himself?'

Ruth pursed her lips. 'I didn't to begin with.'

'But now?'

A slight movement of the head. 'Yes, I think he probably did.'

'Because of what he did to Lauren all those years ago?'

'You know that in the Catholic Church suicide is a mortal sin.'

'I know.'

Ruth crossed herself, just a flick of a wrist across her chest. 'May God have mercy on my soul for saying this, but I hope he killed himself. And I hope he did it because of what he did to Lauren.'

Mark took a sip of his tea, tepid now. He thought about what Ruth had said. Did she really not know what William had been doing? For that matter, did Lauren really not remember until therapy? What if one or both of them had known earlier, before William went missing. He pictured William's decomposed body, face down in the water at Portmore, and felt a shiver move through him.

'There's something else,' Ruth said.

'What?'

'I wasn't entirely truthful when I said that I hadn't heard from Lauren since Nathan's birthday. That was the last time I saw her, but she phoned me more recently.'

63

'When?'

'Two weeks ago.' Ruth was looking out the window again, avoiding him. 'She told me she was pregnant. It was after the scan. She said she was having a baby girl and wanted me to know. She said she was worried.'

Mark moved his hands from the mug to the edge of the table, straightened up.

'Why didn't you say anything before?'

'She told me not to.'

'Why?'

'This isn't easy.'

'Tell me.'

Ruth turned to look him in the eye. 'She said she was worried that she was having a daughter. Specifically a daughter.'

It took a second for Mark to click. 'She thought I might do something to my own daughter?'

Ruth shook her head. 'She never said that. It wasn't rational, she wasn't thinking straight. It was just dark thoughts. Consider what it must be like for her. No one wants to have doubts about their husband, God help me, I know all about that. But after everything she went through with her father, you can't blame her.'

Mark rubbed at his face. 'I can't believe it.'

Now it was Ruth's turn to put out a hand to Mark. He shrugged it off.

'She never doubted you for a second,' Ruth said.

Mark pushed his chair back and stood up.

'Wait, Mark, don't go just yet. We need to talk about this.'

'No, we don't,' Mark said, and headed for the door.

11

His Peugeot rocked in the wind as he thrust the clutch in at the lights and wrestled the gear stick into first. Gearbox was sticking more and more. The cost of keeping it on the road getting ever higher.

Into Porty High Street, Mark checked the clock on the police station. Five minutes to park and get Nathan. He turned down Bath Street rather than Marlborough Street to save time, then met a Tesco van coming the other way and had to pull in. Come on, for Christ's sake.

He got to the bottom of the street, no spaces. Into Straiton Place, eventually he found a place almost at Marlborough Street. Locked up and scuttled along the prom in a half-jog. To his right, the coastguard boat was out again, further from shore this time, only a smudge on the horizon. Maybe the whales weren't doomed after all. Weren't they supposed to be more intelligent than humans?

A sudden drop in the wind and he heard the school bell ring. He was almost there. Round the corner, out of breath, he joined the gaggle of mums in the playground. The classroom door wasn't open yet. He bent over and heaved air into his lungs. Too old for this shit.

The 2B door opened. Nathan was always one of the first to leave. Not today. Mark scanned the kids streaming out, a mess of red uniforms, untucked shirts, lunchboxes and bags swinging. It was like opening the doors of the asylum as the playground filled with yammering noise.

Still no Nathan. Mark clenched his fists and took a step forward. Closed his eyes and opened them again. And there he was, last out, trudging, not the usual sprint, his bottom lip tripping him.

'Hey, Big Guy, what's up?'

'Miss Kennedy wants to speak to you.' Tears were filling his eyes.

Mark went down on his haunches and examined the boy. Gave him a cuddle.

'It's OK, don't worry.'

Nathan hadn't got into full-on crying, just a sniffle. Mark stood up and took his hand.

'Come on, let's go and chat to Miss Kennedy.'

The teacher stood at the classroom door, arms crossed, biting her lip.

'A quick word,' she said, then turned to Nathan. 'Can you wait here for a moment? Thanks.'

Nathan's head sank, like a robot powering down.

'Back in a minute,' Mark said.

Miss Kennedy pulled the door closed. 'We had a bit of a bad day. Nathan was caught hitting. Twice.'

'What?'

'In the classroom. The second time he really clobbered one of the girls at his table.'

'I don't understand. That doesn't sound like him.'

Miss Kennedy unfolded her arms.

'I know, that's why I didn't send him to Mr White's office.'

She tucked her bob behind her ear. 'It's so out of character for Nathan, he's normally quiet and kind.'

Mark shook his head.

Miss Kennedy tilted her head in sympathy. 'Is everything OK at home?'

'What?'

She raised a hand. 'It's none of my business, but Nathan mentioned that his mum wasn't around at the moment?'

It had only been a day and Mark hadn't told him anything. But the boy knew something. The same way Mark knew everything about Nathan, it worked both ways. Kids can sense it. Tension, stress. Mark had to stay on top of this.

'She's just away with work, nothing to worry about.'

'Oh, I must've got the wrong end of the stick,' Miss Kennedy said. 'But perhaps you should have a quiet word with him at home, and we'll both keep an eye on his behaviour for the next wee while. OK?'

She ushered him to leave. He moved towards the door.

'Thanks, I'll speak to him.'

She smiled as she opened the door. 'Don't be too hard on him, he's a lovely wee boy.'

'OK, thanks.'

Nathan glanced up, but kept his chin pointing at the floor. Mark took his hand, felt the little bones under the skin, the delicate knuckle. Gave the hand a squeeze, felt a squeeze back, a little signal between them.

Miss Kennedy shut the door.

Mark turned them towards the prom.

'Let's get you home.'

Nathan stopped. 'No, Daddy, it's Wednesday.'

'And?'

'Swimming lesson.'

Mark shook his head. 'Yeah, of course.'

Nathan's swimming stuff was already packed into his school-bag, Mark had made sure of that this morning. Was that just this morning?

They trudged along the prom into the wind, Mark thinking how to approach the subject of hitting. Or whether to approach it at all.

Instead of turning up Marlborough Street they kept walking along the prom to Porty Baths, a Victorian sandstone building with balconies out front and a huge glass roof.

The changing rooms were the usual chaos of kids and mums. Mark found a cubicle and shuffled Nathan inside. He watched as Nathan got undressed then helped him tie up his swimming shorts.

'So what was that all about today?' he said.

'What?'

'The hitting.'

'It wasn't my fault, Daddy.' Already a strain in the boy's voice. Mark had to cut that off before it escalated.

'I'm not cross, OK? I just want to know what happened.'

Nathan had his head down. 'Emma and Lee said nasty things about me.'

'Like what?'

'They said I was a baby.'

'Why did they say that?'

'Because I'm the youngest in the whole class. And the smallest.'

Mark put his hands on Nathan's bare arms. So thin Mark

could wrap his fingers right the way round easily. He lowered his face to Nathan's and kept his voice quiet.

'Don't you listen to anything Emma and Lee say, OK?' Paused for a response. Didn't get one. 'OK?'

'OK.'

'Of course you're not a baby. But listen. Even if people say bad things about you, you don't hit, you know that. What should you do?'

'Tell Miss Kennedy.' Nathan's voice monotone, almost comically morose.

'That's right, tell Miss Kennedy. You never hit, OK?'

Slight nod of the head. That was the best he was going to get.

Mark helped the boy on with his goggles and they went through to the small pool where the lesson was held.

Mark sat at the side of the pool with the other parents and watched. He was the only dad, the rest mums. He always got looks for that. It was stiflingly humid in here, made your lungs feel heavy and wet just breathing.

Nathan pushed one swimming disc on each arm and got into the pool with the other kids. There were ten in total, some with no discs at all on their arms. The idea was you started with three of these solid foam things on each arm and gradually reduced, a better system than the old armbands. Nathan had been at lessons for years, slow progress, like everything else physical. Still had stabilisers on his bike. The baby of the class. Mark ground his teeth together.

He remembered all the different stages of Nathan with water. At first, not even wanting to put a toe in. Then in the water, but never letting go of Mark. Then after they got over that, he still didn't want to put his head under or jump in. Not a natural swimmer but he was a trier, he plugged away at things until he got there. Mark respected that.

The boy was scooshing happily across the pool on his back now, head pointing up towards the glass roof, thin clouds scudding above. The instructor's voice and the splashing bounced off the tiled walls and floor, drowning everything in a wash of white noise.

Mark sank into the noise and zoned out. Before he knew it, the lesson was almost over, Nathan and the rest lined up for the jumping in they always did at the end. Jump in one at a time and swim to the side. Easy. The instructor took Nathan's remaining discs off. It was always a chance for them to stretch the kids, see how far they could go. But this was the first time Nathan would be in the water with nothing to help him.

Nathan waited his turn then leapt. More of a bellyflop than anything, legs spread. He went under. A couple of seconds' wait. The vague shimmer of his body under the surface. Two more seconds. The instructor was talking to the next kid, not looking at the pool. Another second. Mark was out his seat, only then realising he'd been holding his breath since Nathan went under. Another moment. Mark could see movement under the water. The instructor turned back. Noticed that Nathan hadn't surfaced yet. Leaned over the edge of the pool, lowered the long metal pole he was holding. Mark was several strides towards them now, moving fast, almost running. Then Nathan's head broke the surface, his slick hair, his familiar blue goggles. He was clutching the pole, the instructor dragging it over to the side, helping him. Mark slowed. He could see Nathan was coughing, had swallowed some of the water. But he was OK. He was at the edge of the pool now, clinging on, shuffling sideways towards the steps, ready to come out.

Mark held Nathan's towel out and wrapped him up in it, squeezing the boy through the folds.

The lesson was over, the other kids traipsing back to their mums.

Mark took Nathan's goggles off. Rings around his eyes where the rubber had dug in. The boy was grinning.

'I did it, Daddy, I jumped in with no discs.'

'I saw. You were brilliant.'

Mark led him back to the changing rooms and dried him off in the cubicle, Nathan talking excitedly.

Mark got the boy's clothes from the locker and handed them over. He felt something in the pocket of Nathan's trousers and dug his hand in. Came out with the piece of sea glass. Held it up.

'I thought you were going to put this with the collection?'

Nathan shrugged. 'I decided to keep it in my pocket.'

'Why?'

'I want to wait and show it to Mummy first, before it goes with the rest.'

The sea glass collection was really Nathan's and Lauren's together. One of their joint little things. It was usually Lauren who spotted them, better at searching amongst the finer details of things close at hand. They had a joke that Mark was always staring off into the distance, looking to frame a landscape.

'Fair enough,' Mark said. 'But make sure you don't lose it.'

He put it back in the trouser pocket and passed the trousers to Nathan.

Nathan pushed his legs in.

'I can't wait to tell Mummy I jumped in with no discs. She's going to be so proud of me.'

12

Back in the flat it was unbearable. He checked every room when they got in, nothing had changed, no sign that she'd been home. He opened the underwear drawer, felt the heft of the gun box at the back, but didn't take it out.

He called her phone again. He had a routine now, every hour on the hour. His pulse pounded as he listened to it ringing. She wouldn't answer, but that didn't stop him tensing every sinew in his body with each ring, then crackly silence, then ring, then crackles, then ring. Same voicemail message. He hung up.

As they'd walked up Marlborough Street he had a similar pounding of hope, checking all the cars. But no black Volkswagen Golf. It was a company car, which got him thinking about his visit to the office. That was only this morning. Seemed like a different universe. He thought about Gavin Taylor. Had Ferguson been to speak to him yet?

He flicked up a picture of Lauren on his phone. Just a snapshot, from a rare night out together, in the tapas place round the corner, one of the girls from Nathan's old nursery babysitting for a few hours.

He stroked the screen. Zoomed in. Zoomed in again, to the edge of resolution. Moved the focus around, looked at a green eye with flecks of grey through the iris. The split ends on her auburn hair. Thin lips smiling. Lines around the eyes. Years of love in those eyes. Looking at the individual elements of her face, he struggled to get a sense of her. Was she already fading in his mind?

That night in the restaurant they had mostly talked about Nathan, unable to remember what they did with their time before he arrived. That was before they had baby number two coming. They had quite a bit of red wine, both of them unable to drink like they used to, out of practice and bone-tired from parenthood in a way Mark could never have imagined when he was younger.

They'd also talked about Lauren's work that night. He tried to remember. But the truth was he only half listened when she did shoptalk. She had the usual gripes about colleagues, nothing serious. Just letting off steam. He tried to think what she'd been like before yesterday, before she was gone. What had they last talked about? Was she worried about something?

He screwed his eyes tight and actually rubbed at his temples, like a cheap showbiz mind reader.

He opened his eyes and checked the time. Had an idea.

Went through to the living room, where Nathan was plugged into *Horrid Henry* on CITV.

'Come on, we're going out.'

'Aw, I'm watching telly.'

'You can play your DS in the car.'

That knocked him into shape. The telly was off in a moment and he was trotting behind Mark towards the door.

'Where are we going?'

They were at the door when Mark thought of something. 'Hang on.'

He went to Nathan's room and opened the cupboard door. A pile of toys stacked up in a heap on top of a set of drawers full of more of the boy's junk. He pulled open the first drawer, knew what he was looking for and found it straight away. Nathan's *Star Wars* binoculars. Or 'optical command unit' as they were officially called. The kind Luke uses in the first film to search for R2-D2. A favourite from a year ago. Nathan used to sleep with them under his pillow. As Mark remembered it, they were actually half-decent binoculars. He stuck them in his pocket and headed for the door.

13

He stopped on a double yellow line two hundred yards down the road from the office, handbrake on, engine off. The sounds of rush-hour traffic trundling across the cobbles, the wind making the car squeak and rattle, lightsaber and blaster noises coming from Nathan's DS. The boy hadn't lifted his head the entire journey. It had taken Mark longer than expected from Porty, a busier time of day than before.

He focused the toy binoculars on the Caledonia Dreaming front door, then looked at his phone. Ten to five. While he had his phone out, he checked Lauren's Facebook and Twitter again. Nothing. It already had the air of a ritual, something in the phoning and the checking, attempting to conjure her back into their lives with the routine of it.

Nathan hadn't even noticed they'd stopped. Mark stared at him in the back seat, the boy's head down, thumbs flicking over the DS controls.

'What level are you on?' Mark said.

Nathan talked for a full two minutes without seemingly taking a breath or lifting his head, his thumbs still jerking around. Mark had little idea what any of it meant, occasionally catching a name like 'General Grievous' or 'Mace Windu'. But he just enjoyed drowning in the sound of the boy's voice, his simple enthusiasm for an alien universe.

Mark trained the binoculars back on the office and spotted the young receptionist leaving, battling into the wind as she tried to look cool in big red heels. She walked up the hill towards George Street. Mark got a good view of her as she walked, the binoculars were not too bad at all.

A few minutes later Taylor was in the doorway, punching numbers into a security alarm, then pulling the heavy door closed and turning the chunky mortice.

He walked fifty yards to a silver Lexus saloon and got in. Mark threw the binoculars on the passenger seat and started the engine. The Lexus pulled out and Mark did likewise, following him up to Queen Street then turning.

Mark tried to keep him in view, but was held up by the relentless roadworks. Eventually he was clear on Lothian Road and spotted the Lexus up ahead, then into Tollcross, round the Meadows and through Marchmont towards the Grange. On to Oswald Road and the Lexus turned into the driveway of a large villa, black stone recently cleaned and pointed. Hefty wooden kids' swing and slide set in the front garden. Mark pulled over some way back up the street and killed the engine.

He watched as Taylor locked the car, went up the steps and in the front door. Saw him call out hellos as he closed the door behind him.

Mark decided to wait for ten minutes, so it wouldn't seem like he'd been following him. Maybe. He spent the time scanning the house and garden with the binoculars, examining the stonework and the expensive curtains.

Eventually he turned to Nathan. 'I'll be back in a minute, OK?'

Nathan raised his head. 'Where are we?'

'I just have to go and talk to a friend for a second.'

'Do I have to come?' Reluctant to leave the game.

'No, just wait here, I'll be back in a bit.'

'OK.'

More lightsaber swishes, a few bars of the *Star Wars* theme in the background, tinny and grating.

Mark left the car and walked up the drive. Glanced back at Nathan, head down. He went up the steps and stood at the entrance. Etched glass in the door, a picture of ducks on water. Probably Blackford Pond round the corner. Clearly the property business was treating Taylor very well indeed. Much better than Lauren anyway.

Mark rang the doorbell.

A girl opened the door. She was a couple of years older than Nathan, in a Heriot's uniform, hair in plaits.

'Yes?'

'Is your daddy home?'

The girl turned. 'Dad?'

She was too old for 'Daddy'. Mark wondered when that would happen to Nathan.

The girl disappeared and Taylor arrived at the door.

'What are you doing here?' He stepped outside and pulled the door behind him.

'I just wondered if you'd heard anything from Lauren.'

Taylor stared at him. 'Why are you at my home?'

'I need to find Lauren. Have you heard anything?'

Taylor pointed a stubby finger at Mark's chest. 'You need to get a grip of yourself. You can't go pestering people like this.'

'There's no law against it.'

'There is, it's called stalking.'

'I need to find her.'

'I don't know anything more than I told you this morning. Oh, and thanks for sending the police to the office as well.'

'It's routine in missing person cases.'

Taylor shook his head. 'She's only been gone a day. Maybe she just needed time away from your paranoia.'

Mark could hear kids shouting and giggling inside, clumpy footsteps on solid stairs.

'Nice family you've got,' he said.

Taylor was backing into the house. 'Go home, Mark. And don't come to my house again.'

'Are you threatening me?'

Taylor had the door half shut. 'Just go.'

The door closed. Mark stared at the etched glass and imagined how easy it would be to get a stone and smash the window.

14

It wasn't a bath night, but he hustled Nathan into the tub anyway. Anything to keep occupied. Little ducks and submarines, a drinking straw they took turns with, seeing how big a bubble they could make. Nathan had carefully placed the sea glass on the edge of the bath.

The boy had already asked about Lauren, of course. Mark said she was away working for a few days. It had happened once or twice before, conferences or properties at the other end of the country to visit, so it wasn't too much of a stretch. Nathan wanted to know why she hadn't called, though. She always called before bedtime. Maybe her phone needed charging up, another familiar scenario, she was always forgetting. With each little lie, he felt the universe closing in on him, the wind outside trying to make him pay for what he said by pushing their windows in.

'How's your tooth?' he said.

Nathan put a hand to his mouth, gave a shoogle. His eyes widened and became watery as he pulled his fist away with a tiny milk tooth in it. Blood was pooling on his tongue and dripping off his lip into the bathwater. He made a gurgling sound. There was a lot of blood. Why the hell was it bleeding? Surely they just came out no problem, didn't they?

Mark grabbed some toilet roll and spun a wad into his hand,

holding it against Nathan's mouth. The boy's eyes were blazing with surprise.

'Daddy?' he said through the paper. 'Why's it bleeding?'

'It's fine.' Mark folded the blood-soaked side of the paper under and reapplied the wad. 'It'll stop in a second. Sometimes baby teeth bleed a little when they come out.'

Nathan shrugged. Matter-of-fact. Still young enough to take what Mark told him on trust.

The bleeding had reduced to a trickle already, and Mark dabbed the paper against the gum and lip, mopping up what was left. The bathwater had a few swirls of red amongst the bubbles, little threads of life through the soap.

He checked the bleeding had stopped. Nathan was still holding the tiny tooth like a diamond between thumb and forefinger.

'How much do you think the tooth fairy will give me for it?'

Mark sucked his tongue. 'Well, it's a cracker, so quite a lot.'

He had no idea what the going rate was, this was Nathan's first and he didn't have any comparison.

Nathan scrambled out of the bath, still clutching the tooth, and Mark began drying him. The boy could do it himself, but Mark wanted to. He ran his eyes over Nathan's body. There was something unbearably pure and beautiful about it, the skinny ribs, the slender limbs. His knees and shins were covered in bruises, Nathan had the typical little-boy tactic of running until he hit something. Looked like abuse if you didn't know better. Mark rubbed him dry then patted his bum.

'Go get your jammies on, Big Guy.'

Mark stood with the damp towel against his face for a

minute, imagining being suffocated, then got Nathan's tooth-brush ready and went through to his bedroom.

The boy was already in bed with his tooth in one hand and the piece of sea glass in the other. Like a witch doctor with a pair of ancient talismans. *The Cat in the Hat* was lying on his lap.

Mark handed over the toothbrush.

'Just gently, and leave the front, no point making it bleed again.'

Nathan was buzzing with excitement about the tooth. 'Just wait till I tell Ahmed tomorrow. Did you know, Daddy, Ahmed got two pounds for his tooth last week.'

At least Mark knew the going rate now. He wondered if he had two quid in change in the house. Might have to take it out of Nathan's piggy bank once he was asleep.

Nathan finished brushing and put the tooth under his pil-low. He kept hold of the sea glass. Mark started reading the book. Nathan was almost too old for Dr Seuss, but Mark was glad he still liked it. There was no gender-divide bullshit with these books, so different from modern kids' stuff. And what was the moral of *The Cat in the Hat*? Let chaos into your life, embrace it, and everything will be all right in the end. And remember to keep it all a secret from your parents. Great.

He tucked Nathan in and left the bedside light on.

'I can't wait to tell Mummy about the tooth,' Nathan said.

Mark put on a smile and left the room.

What now?

He got a beer from the fridge, slugged it. Sat down at the laptop and decided to bite the bullet. He posted up on Face-book and Twitter that Lauren was missing. He hadn't wanted to do that in the beginning, but there seemed no alternative now. Got a couple of quick comments on Facebook from people offering generic support, nothing useful. A few retweets on Twitter, nothing else.

He spent the next three hours searching 'Lauren Bell' in Google and other search engines, different variations and combinations. Nothing new in the last few weeks, just lots of old shit.

It didn't make him feel any better, but at least he was doing something. The only other thing he could think of to do was to go into the streets and look for her himself. But he had Nathan in the next room, that wasn't an option.

So where did that leave him? Exactly where he was when she hadn't turned up at Towerbank yesterday. Only yesterday. Seemed like weeks ago.

He stuck on the television as he sucked on his third beer. All the same old stuff. Channels were still broadcasting, the world still turning, but Lauren was gone. He felt rage build up in him, at her for disappearing, at the world for not giving a shit, at Nathan for blindly believing his lies about everything.

He remembered about the tooth fairy and went through to the kitchen. Found a two-pound coin in the drawer where they sometimes threw their change. Lucky. Snuck into Nathan's room and switched it for the tooth. It was tiny, didn't look any use for biting or chewing or anything. What was he supposed to do with it now? What did you do with your kids' baby teeth? He should probably keep it somewhere safe. Another thing Lauren would know about.

He slipped the tooth into his pocket, pulled Nathan's covers over his bare arms and stood watching him for a while. Fast, shallow breathing, like a puppy. Pale skin, almost grey in the half-light. A slight smell came off him, every night the same, something vaguely feral. Earthy. Not at all unpleasant.

Mark needed a piss and went to the toilet. The bathwater was still in the tub, cloudy with soap and dirt and slightly pink from Nathan's blood. Mark reached over and pulled the plug, collecting all the bath toys up. He picked a towel off the floor and hung it up. He noticed three spots of blood on it, then looked at the floor. Several more dark droplets glistening on the laminate. Nathan's mouth must've bled longer than he realised.

He thought of when Lauren's waters broke, blood spotting amongst the splash on the kitchen floor, her pants soaked through. He remembered the drive to hospital, over the high road past Craigmillar Castle to ERI, then the long wait, Lauren's pain in sweeping waves, his inability to help, his feelings of rage and impotence at what she was going through.

It wasn't an easy birth. Twenty-seven hours of labour, contractions stopping and starting, Lauren gradually getting ground down by it, weaker and weaker as she got more exhausted from the whole ordeal. Then, just as they were talking about a C-section, the contractions kicked up a notch and it was happening, Mark sidelined as the midwives did their thing, Lauren's face plastered with sweat and anguish and a raw panic he'd never seen in her before.

Nathan was a healthy size and breathing but Lauren was in trouble. She wouldn't stop bleeding afterwards. The midwives gave up looking calm and a doctor was called. The baby was handed to Mark to keep them both out the way, the focus on Lauren. The doctor and three midwives were all talking at once.

The doctor injected something into Lauren's leg then began pushing at her abdomen. That couldn't be good. One of the midwives said that anything over 500 ml was technically a haemorrhage. Lauren had lost a litre and a half of blood, soaking red paper towels piling up in a corner of the room. Lauren's painkillers kicked in and she looked semi-catatonic as Mark watched, the panic in him now, feeling the tiny weight of Nathan in his arms as everyone fussed over the lower half of Lauren's body. Mark heard the doctor mention the possibility of surgery. Someone else arrived with blood packs and hooked up Lauren's arm for transfusion.

But then somehow, gradually, the bleeding subsided. The staff stepped down from high alert and the doctor said some reassuring words to him and Lauren, none of which they could remember afterwards. It wasn't even clear what the problem had been, and they never thought to ask, so relieved that they were all still in one piece, with their new baby gurgling away, scrunching up his nose and waving his fists at the world.

The same boy who, now, was growing up and losing his baby teeth.

Mark got the tooth out his pocket and gave it a rub. Was that lucky? Was that a thing, to rub a milk tooth and make a wish? He thought about the baby inside Lauren right now. He made a wish anyway, lucky or not.

He walked back to the living room and checked the laptop. Nothing had changed online.

The late-night news was on the television. He wanted to see a big picture of Lauren appear, one of the ones he'd emailed to Ferguson earlier. He thought about phoning her, her mobile number was on the card in his pocket, but it was already after midnight.

Some footage from Porty beach came on the television. Mark turned the volume up. The voiceover said the pod of pilot whales were making their way to the mouth of the Forth, heading for open water. It looked like they were going to be safe. All that worry and effort over nothing. The whales had decided not to kill themselves. The voiceover said the coastguard was remaining cautious, though, until the whales were completely out to sea.

Mark closed his eyes and imagined being out there with them, slinking through the freezing North Sea, blue-green swells like a blanket around him.

15

He was woken by screaming. He bolted off the sofa and scrambled through to Nathan's room, where the boy was thrashing around on top of his covers, wailing like a baby and holding his hands out as if trying to ward off evil spirits. It was like he was having a fit, but then his eyes shot open and the screaming turned to plain crying.

Mark sat on the edge of the bed, buffeted by Nathan's still flailing legs.

'Shhh, it's OK, Big Guy.' He kept his voice low, stroked the boy's head and held his shoulders. 'You just had a bad dream. It's OK, nothing to be afraid of. Daddy's here, OK? Daddy's here.'

The crying reduced to a whimper, but Nathan's breath was still catching in his chest, and he stuttered as he tried to breathe, shudders passing through his body as he stopped kicking out and his body slackened.

Mark pulled him into a tight cuddle and made soft, reassuring noises, like trying to calm an animal caught in a trap.

He fought the urge to ask about the bad dream. He wanted to know what it was about, but what good would it do to bring it up? He felt his own chest heave a few times as he clutched at the boy's back, trying to keep his own nightmares at bay.

He let Nathan go, and the boy sat up. Mark handed him a

tissue and he wiped at the tear tracks on his cheeks, then blew his nose, sniffing afterwards half a dozen times. He seemed ultra-awake now, aware of the details of his surroundings. Mark checked the bedside clock, quarter to two.

'Can I sleep in your bed, Daddy?'

'You're a bit old for that.' Lauren had always indulged him more on that front, but he hadn't been into their bed in over a year.

'Please.'

What the hell did it matter? Plenty of room in the marital bed tonight anyway.

'Sure, why not.'

Nathan trotted down the hall, dragging a ragged old teddy by the leg. By the time Mark was in the room, Nathan was already tucked in and lying on his side, watching as Mark undressed to his shorts and T-shirt.

He got under the covers and spooned the boy, who made a little contented snuffle. Mark felt the sharpness of the boy's corners, his growing bones jutting out all over the place. Compared it to Lauren's curves, couldn't help himself.

Nathan turned his head. 'Daddy, is Mummy going to be home soon?' His voice was sleepy.

'Shhh, don't worry about that. Just go back to sleep.'

'She left us before, didn't she?'

'What?'

'She left us one time before.'

Mark propped his head up on his elbow to look at Nathan's face, but the boy was lying with his eyes closed.

'What makes you say that?'

'Mummy told me.'

'When was this?'

'I can't remember.'

Mark put a hand on Nathan's shoulder. 'Nathan, this might be important. Was it recently?'

Nathan's eyes were open now, and he frowned.

'I don't know.'

'Try to remember.'

He began to look distressed, a little furrow across his brow. 'I don't know. Not too long ago, I think.'

Mark ran a hand through the boy's hair. 'OK, Big Guy, forget about it just now.'

Nathan lowered his head on to Lauren's pillow. 'So has she left us again, Daddy?'

Mark waited a long time before speaking, feeling his breath, his chest rising and falling, pushing against Nathan's spine. He stroked at the boy's forehead and temple.

'Just go to sleep.'

16

He was trapped inside a whale's stomach, the acid in its belly eating away at his skin and flesh until he was just a skeleton smeared with the remains of his own body. Strange thing was, it didn't hurt.

Then there was a noise. He snapped awake. Years of listening out for Nathan in the night had trained him to sleep lightly. His hand shot out to Nathan, who was lying at a wonky angle across Lauren's side of the bed. The boy was still asleep, chest rising and falling, mouth slack.

Greyness seeped through the curtains in the pre-dawn.

Another noise. From the living room. He recognised the sound, it was a drawer of the desk being opened.

Lauren was home.

His heart thudded against his ribs as he threw off the covers, stumbled out the door and down the hall. He heard a couple of footsteps as he sped past the front door, slightly ajar. He was at the living-room doorway, thinking what to say to her, how to get across the tumbling relief and anger, when he stopped.

At the desk was a large man dressed in a dark hoodie pulled tight over his head, torch in one hand. Paperwork from open drawers was scattered across the floor and the guy was hunting through the last drawer.

Mark couldn't think what to do or say for a moment.

The man turned. He pointed the torch at Mark's face so that Mark couldn't make anything out. Mark raised a hand to shield his eyes and caught a glimpse of the man lifting the laptop out of the bottom drawer. Before Mark had a chance to think, the man was at the doorway. Mark saw a flash as the torch connected with his head. A hammer of pain across his temple and tears sprang to his eyes. He grabbed the doorframe to steady himself, and the man shoved past him and out, down the hall and through the front door.

Mark fell to his knees. He felt sick. His legs shook and he blinked back tears. He lifted a hand to his head and it came away bloody. Just a trickle. Shards of pain shot through his head and down his right arm. He'd only been hit once, but it hurt like hell. He could feel a thread of blood running down the side of his face from a cut just above his right eye.

He heaved himself to his feet and went to the bathroom, put the light on and looked at the cut. Hardly anything. He dabbed at it with some toilet roll and wiped his tears away.

'Is that blood, Daddy?'

He knocked over a cup of toothbrushes that clattered into the bath, the noise shocking in the tiny space.

Nathan was standing at the doorway.

'Are you hurt?'

'I just had a wee accident. Nothing to worry about.'

His hand shook as he raised it to the cut. He ushered the boy out of the bathroom and towards the bedroom.

'Go back to sleep.'

'But I'm not tired now.'

'Just get into bed.' His voice was louder than it needed to be as he nudged Nathan towards the door.

'Ow,' Nathan said. 'That hurt.'

Mark sighed. 'Just please go back to bed.'

'But I want to stay up with you.'

'I'll be through in a minute. If you don't get more sleep, you won't have enough energy for school.'

Nathan stopped in the hall. 'I don't think I'll be well enough for school, Daddy. I have a sore tummy. I feel sick.'

Mark's own stomach was churning.

'Never mind that, just do as you're told. I'll be through in a minute. I have to do something first.'

'What?'

'Just do it.' He was shouting now. He raised a quivering hand to his forehead, took a shaky breath.

Nathan slouched away and climbed up into Mark and Lauren's bed. Mark followed, crouched by the bed and stroked the boy's head.

'I'm sorry for shouting, Big Guy.'

'It's OK, Daddy. I know you miss Mummy when she's away. I miss her too.'

Mark felt Nathan's hand patting his own. Then suddenly Nathan pulled away, his eyes wide.

'Daddy, I forgot something.'

'What?'

Nathan sprang up and bolted out the bedroom and down the hall towards his own room. Mark followed slowly and met him in the hallway coming back. The boy was smiling widely and holding something up.

'Look, the tooth fairy's been.'

'Wow, cool.'

'And I got two pounds, just like Ahmed.'

'That's great.'

Nathan clutched the coin as Mark shepherded him back into his and Lauren's bed. He lay there beaming. So easily pleased.

Mark tucked him in and kissed his forehead. 'Back in a minute.'

In the hall he looked at the front door. The lock was jimmied, splinters on the carpet. He should've noticed it before. He didn't touch it.

He went through to the living room and flicked the light on. Same mess as before, paperwork everywhere. Laptop gone.

He went back to the bedroom and dug Ferguson's card out of his jeans pocket. He went to the wardrobe and opened the underwear drawer, careful to keep his back to Nathan. He felt inside. The Browning was still there. He ran his fingers along the edge of the box, tried the lid. Still locked. He closed the drawer. Turned to see Nathan watching him in the half-light.

'Just need to phone someone,' he said, leaving the room.

He dialled the number. It rang and rang. He was just about to hang up when she answered.

'I've been burgled,' he said.

'I'm sorry, who is this?'

'Mark Douglas, you were here in my flat. My wife is missing.'

'Mr Douglas, it's five in the morning.'

'I've just been robbed.'

'Are you OK?'

'Someone broke into the flat, went through all our stuff and stole our laptop.'

'If there's no immediate danger, phone the station, Mr Douglas, this is a situation for them. Otherwise it's 999.'

'You think it's a coincidence?'

'What?'

'He was going through our desk then took the laptop. This has something to do with Lauren's disappearance.'

'You don't know that.'

Mark shook his head. 'I do.'

'Mr Douglas, people get burgled all the time, it's most likely a coincidence. Now please contact the station, they'll send an officer round when they can.'

'Why did you give me your mobile number, if that's all you've got to say?'

He hung up and called the police station.

17

Nathan was dragging his heels more than usual, complaining about a sore tummy, having to be pulled along the prom to Towerbank. Thank Christ the wind seemed to have died down for now. Maybe they were in the eye of the storm. Mark had stared at the weather forecast on television earlier but now couldn't remember a word of it, just swirls of arrows pointing across the country.

They were late. Nathan had eventually gone back to sleep then slept in as a result, and Mark didn't have the heart to wake him. Mark made his packed lunch and got his stuff together while Nathan slept on, then eventually Mark shoogled him awake and rushed through breakfast and dressing to get out the door, Nathan running back to his bedroom to get the sea glass and put it in his pocket.

Mark hadn't gone back to sleep after the break-in. The station said they would send an officer as soon as they could, but there was no immediate danger and they didn't seem in a hurry. They talked about manpower issues, as if Mark gave two shits.

Either way, an officer hadn't turned up by the time they left for school. The lock on the front door was hanging off, but Mark didn't try to fix it in case the police wanted to look at it, dust for prints, whatever. He pulled the door closed but it was only an illusion of security, a gentle nudge would've swung it open. He would have to deal with it after the school run. He'd go to the station straight after dropping Nathan off. Surely they would have to do something now.

The prom was a relief after the crazy winds of the last few days. The sun was already high in the sky behind them, and the water of the Forth was a slab of shimmering silver. No sign of the whales or the coastguard, maybe they'd finally swum out to sea.

Nathan was griping as they trudged along, no bins out today to shoot at and distract him. This wasn't like him these days, more like P1 behaviour, but he was obviously picking up the stress from Daddy. Mark touched the cut above his eye, already scabbing over, hardly anything to show.

He'd sat waiting for the police, watching the sun nudge upwards from the kitchen window, the tiny sliver of sea barely distinguishable from the pale sky. Tried to figure out what the intruder meant. He didn't want to go through all the mess on the floor, not until the police had been, so he didn't know if there was anything specific gone – but what could they have taken? There was nothing in the desk except standard family paperwork. The guy had taken the laptop, but that was the only piece of electronics as far as Mark knew. He'd left all Mark's camera equipment, worth a small fortune in the right hands. Hadn't touched the television either, but then that was harder to carry and Mark had interrupted him after all.

Nathan was going slower than ever.

Mark tugged the boy's arm. 'Come on, Nathan.'

Nathan planted his feet and came to a standstill.

Mark gave him a look. 'You're not a baby, stop acting like one.'

Nathan's face was sour.

'What is it?' Mark said.

'Is Mummy gone because she's got a new baby in her tummy?'

'What?'

'She's got a new baby in her tummy. Is that why she's gone?'

'How do you know about that?'

'She told me.'

That wasn't the plan. They weren't supposed to have told anyone yet, they'd only just got the all-clear at the scan a couple of weeks ago. So Lauren had told Ruth without him knowing, and now she'd told Nathan as well.

He looked at his watch. 'We don't have time for this, we're late for school. Miss Kennedy will be cross.'

He went to grab the boy's hand, but Nathan pulled away.

'Come on,' Mark shouted. 'I'm getting angry now. Let's go.'

Nothing.

Mark knelt down to Nathan's eye level. Tried to stay calm. 'It's nothing to do with that. I told you, Mummy is working away from home for a few days, that's all.'

What was Lauren playing at, telling Nathan about the new baby without discussing it with him first? Jesus.

Mark coaxed the boy forward, one reluctant step after another. They eventually got to the lane between the amusements and the play park where they turned up for school. Mark heard the bell go.

He pulled Nathan along. 'Come on.'

The boy shuffled forward, and as they turned the corner they saw the end of 2B's line scuffing its way into the classroom.

Miss Kennedy was standing with her arms crossed at the door, fielding six-year-old chatter with a smile.

Mark handed Nathan his lunchbox.

'Kiss.'

Nathan kissed him and Mark felt the dry skin of the boy's lips. Forgot to put Vaseline on them again. They'd be a cut-up mess pretty soon at this rate.

He patted Nathan on the bottom, more like a shove. 'On you go. Have fun.'

Nathan stumbled forward as the last of the stragglers bundled into the class. Miss Kennedy waved him over and he sped up. She held the door for him as he scuttled inside, then smiled at Mark and closed the door.

Mark stood with the sun on his face, the playground suddenly silent after the mayhem of kid noise. He soaked in the warmth for a moment, tried to empty his mind. He had to get the police round to the flat, check what was missing. Then he had to get a locksmith for the door.

His phone rang. The screen said it was Fletcher from the picture desk at the *Standard*. Mark had switched all his shifts for the next few days, couldn't handle working with Lauren gone. He hadn't told anyone at work the reason. Fletcher obviously hadn't got the message. Mark answered.

'I'm not working today.'

'You live in Porty, right? Are you anywhere near the beach just now?'

'I'm not working today.'

'Just yes or no.'

'Yes.'

'Get your gear and get down to the east end. We've got a report of a body washed up on the shore.'

'You mean one of the pilot whales?'

'No. A woman.'

18

He ran.

He ran until his chest burned and his legs turned to liquid and all he could hear was his own heartbeat thundering in his head, until it felt like all the blood in his body would burst out his veins at once. He ran past the bottom of Marlborough Street and on, feet slapping on the prom, past the swimming baths and the flats.

He could see something past the next groyne. The tide was way out, a hundred yards of wet sand in its wake. Half a dozen people were standing in a huddle, unnaturally close together, uncomfortable stances, two of them holding each other.

He sprinted on to the beach, kicking up sand that filled his shoes, the heavy going sucking strength from his legs. He scrambled over the groyne, scraped his shin on the rough wood, staggered on, squelching and splashing through the puddles under his feet now, his vision blurred with the strain.

Some of the crowd turned and separated as they heard him approach. Behind them he caught a glimpse of something, a black shape, glistening wet in the sunlight, partly covered in a thin smear of sand.

He stumbled and fell, pushed himself back up into a crouching run. He tried to remember again what Lauren had been wearing when she went out the door of the flat that morning.

Then he saw the body on the ground more clearly and recognised the curve of the hip, a curve he'd admired and touched for eighteen years, Lauren's hip, in the A-line skirt she was wearing to work two days ago. Thick tights covering her legs, he could see them now, she'd worn them even though it was springtime, he always took the piss out of her for feeling the cold so badly. And the simple black jacket she always wore to work, the kind of smart thing they never could've imagined her wearing when they'd first met as clubbing teenagers.

He reached the crowd, which parted in front of him. As if they knew. He skidded to his knees beside the body. She was facing away from him, looking out towards the sea. He turned her over.

Lauren.

Her skin was blue and grey, eyes closed. He touched her cheek. It was so cold, it didn't feel like skin at all. Didn't feel human.

He grabbed her shoulders and hauled her up off the claggy sand into a hug, gripping her tight, feeling the cold sponginess of her body, tasting salt in his mouth. He stroked her wet hair, knotted and tuggy, and pictured that expensive conditioner she used in the bath.

His body began to shake and he worried that he was going to drop her on to the sand, which seemed more awful than anything. The spasms convulsed through his muscles and he struggled to breathe, as if he'd been winded. He tried to gasp air into his lungs but he couldn't. His eyes were blind with tears and snot ran from his nose. He couldn't get snot on her, but he couldn't let go either. He leaned away for a second and wiped his nose on his sleeve. He clutched her to his chest again, couldn't stand to see her face. It was easier to hold her than look at her. He finally got a stuttering breath into his lungs and an ugly wail crept out of him.

He sat with her like that for a lifetime, his mind dead, his body shaking, his blood cold and congealed in his veins.

'Mark?'

From the bottom of the ocean, he somehow felt a hand on his shoulder. He drifted upwards towards reality, then broke the surface.

'Mark.'

The hand tried to turn him, but he held on to Lauren like a shipwreck survivor clinging to driftwood. If he could just keep holding her, he could stay afloat.

The hand was removed from his shoulder, then he sensed someone in front of him. He opened his eyes and saw a face he recognised, features he could place but somehow different, as if the whole world had been shunted off kilter.

'It's me, DC Ferguson. Tracey?'

There were other police officers behind her, and an ambulance crew. He raised his head to look around. A smudge of faces and limbs, murmuring voices, the swish of the tide lapping a few feet away. The stench of salt water choked everything, corroding the world.

'Mark, the paramedics need to check her over. You have to let go.'

He resisted his fingers being prised away from Lauren's back, then finally gave in and slumped on to the sand. Two men in medical uniforms crouched next to Lauren. Mark imagined them giving her mouth-to-mouth, pumping away at her chest until she spluttered back to life, coughing up seawater like in the movies. But they were just methodically checking her neck, heart, eyes, ears. Like livestock at market. They conferred quietly between themselves then stepped away.

He scrambled back to her, leaned over. Stroked her cheek, her brow. The truth was, since Nathan had come along, they hadn't had the time or energy to touch each other or really look closely at each other any more like they used to at the start. This would be the last time he would ever look at her face. He wanted to see her eyes open, but at the same time he was terrified by the idea, how final that would be to see her lifeless gaze.

He tucked a strand of hair behind her ear. She always fussed about her hair getting in her face, tying it back more often than not, especially at work. Had it been tied back when she left the house two days ago?

His tears were falling on her face and he wiped them away in a shameful panic, feeling the slackness of her skin, a kind of rubbery oiliness. He felt tremors starting up in his arms and legs and he hunched forward, head on the sand. He wanted the beach to choke him to death. He wanted the sand to scour his eyes and block his nose, he wanted the sea to drag him under, annihilate him.

'Come on.'

It was Ferguson again, trying to get him to sit up.

Mark looked at Lauren and suddenly felt sick, a spasm rushing up from his stomach. He retched on the sand, tears and snot dripping, his body convulsing. He could feel Ferguson's hand rubbing his back, and all he could think was how pointless that touch was, how completely pointless.

19

Back at the police station. No idea how he got here. Same dismal grey walls, same crime-prevention posters with the stupid slogans, even the same spotty kid behind the desk.

Except it wasn't the same, nothing would ever be the same again. Sunlight was glinting in through the glass door of the building, and Mark could see leaves and litter being tossed around in a swirl outside. Wind must be picking up again.

He closed his eyes and saw Lauren's face. Cold and blue, lips dry, those lines around her eyes like cracks in concrete. He tried to picture her the morning she disappeared but he couldn't conjure anything up, couldn't get an image of her alive. Was this how it was going to be? Was the memory of her already dead?

He flicked through his phone, looked at a couple of pictures of her with Nathan, crappy little snaps, one at a birthday party, two from a trip to the zoo months ago. All the everyday family stuff that was never going to happen again.

Fuck, he'd have to tell Nathan. He felt sick. Couldn't picture the scenario at all, impossible to contemplate.

Every minute since she hadn't turned up at Towerbank, he'd presumed she would be back. He'd panicked and fussed and worried but deep in his core, he always thought she'd come walking through the door after a while, like last time. They would carry on like they had before, struggling, sure, but making it work.

But not now. Not ever.

He thought about the unborn child inside her. Shame came pouring into him that he'd only thought of that now. Every single one of his thoughts and actions now was an insult to Lauren, the baby, himself, Nathan, the world.

Ferguson appeared in front of him, blocking the light from the door. She held a mug out to him.

'Tea. I put some sugar in it.'

Sugary tea, Jesus fucking Christ. Another insult. How could the world put up with this degradation?

He stared at the whispers of steam coming from the mug. Ferguson put it down on a low table covered with leaflets. Neighbourhood Watch. Community Policing.

'I know this is hard,' she said.

'Do you.'

'I just need to go through a couple of things with you.'

Mark rubbed at his eye then made a gesture with his hand, letting her continue.

'This is ridiculous, but I need you to verbally confirm that was your wife Lauren Bell on the beach.'

Mark's eyelids flickered involuntarily. 'Yes, that's her.' He was aware as he spoke that he'd used the present tense, not the past. Not ready for that shift, not yet.

'Can you remember if that's what she was wearing when you last saw her?'

Mark closed his eyes this time, tried to think. Pictured her walking into the living room with a piece of toast in her hand.

Never still, no one was ever stationary in the mornings in their flat, always running around.

'I think so. She had her hair tied back in a ponytail, though. Is that important?'

Ferguson looked at him kindly. 'It could be.'

Mark got a sudden flash of her lying on the sand. 'Wait. She wasn't wearing any shoes on the beach, why wasn't she wearing any shoes?'

'It doesn't necessarily mean anything. Can you remember what kind of shoes she was wearing?'

He couldn't. Probably heels, maybe strappy. Who the hell notices their wife's shoes after nine years of marriage? More guilt swamped him, suddenly drowning him in sorrow and self-pity. He shook his head, a tiny movement, as if worried he might upset the equilibrium of the earth with the motion.

Too late for that, far too late.

A thought came swimming out the darkness.

'Where is she now?'

Ferguson sat down next to him and placed a hand on his wrist. Mark stared at it. Freckled, delicate, like bird bones. It looked like it could snap too easily.

'They've taken her body to the mortuary on the Cowgate. They'll perform a post-mortem there.'

'When?'

'Depends on the workload, but hopefully soon.'

Workload. To some knife-wielding arsehole in scrubs Lauren was just workload. Another day at the fucking office.

'And then what?'

'Depends on the result of the post-mortem. Whether they declare it an accidental death or . . .'

Mark looked up and held her gaze. 'Or?'

'Suicide. Or murder.'

Mark pulled his hand away from hers and gripped his knees. 'I don't think I can handle this.'

He could sense Ferguson's eyes on him and felt like he was suffocating. He could hear the police officer breathing through her nose and had a sudden urge to choke her.

'I need to know what happened to her,' he said.

'We'll do our best to find out, I promise.'

It was empty, just words. She didn't care, why should she? Just another person clocking in and clocking out. Lauren was another addition to the workload.

'I'm going to find out what happened,' Mark said.

'Please leave the investigating to us.'

Mark concentrated on his own breath, suddenly aware of the particles of air being sucked into his lungs, reacting in there, absorbed into his bloodstream.

Ferguson spoke again. 'Do you have anyone you need to call? A relative?'

He felt his blood sing in his veins, every cell active and alert to possibilities.

'Lauren's mother.'

'Do you want me to inform her about what's happened?'

He shook his head. 'I'll do it.'

'If you're sure.'

He stood up and flicked through his phone. Pressed 'call'. Ruth picked up after two rings. Mark didn't wait for her to speak.

'She's dead,' he said.

20

The Beach House was a mistake. Young mums with toddlers and babies filled the cafe, like some upscale lifestyle advert. The affluent middle classes of Portobello out enjoying their frappuccinos while their hubbies were off earning, mums swapping gossip and calmly managing the chaos of their kids. It seemed to Mark as if it was all an elaborate front, they weren't really human at all, like *Invasion of the Body Snatchers*.

Ruth sat opposite him. She seemed older than when he'd last seen her, but then so did the rest of the world. Everything was broken or decaying now, without purpose.

He felt an urge to speak, but at the same time he couldn't think of a single thing worth saying.

Ruth's face was puffy from crying. They'd hugged awkwardly when she came in, holding on to each other for dear life, a release of tears from them both. Mark didn't know how long they stood like that, but there were plenty of strange looks from the staff and the mums as the sobs escaped.

That release was eventually replaced by numbness as they sat down and ordered drinks. As if their worlds hadn't just ended.

Mark looked around him. Cute little seascapes lined the walls in deliberately distressed white wood frames, artificially weathered. He caught a glimpse of his own reflection in the window. He had a similar weather-beaten look himself.

Ruth nursed a peppermint tea. Mark had a black coffee un-touched in front of him, stone cold.

'I can't believe it,' Ruth said. 'My little girl.'

Mark couldn't think of anything to say that wasn't insulting to the universe.

Ruth looked out the window with a tissue pressed to her nose.

'How, Mark?'

Mark shook his head. 'I don't know.'

'What did the police say?'

'They're waiting on the post-mortem.'

Ruth turned to him. 'Do you think she . . . ?'

Mark knew what she was asking. Did her only daughter kill herself. He wished he could give an answer that wouldn't break her heart even more.

'I don't know.'

Ruth was in tears again, head in her hands, sobs escaping.

'I have to know what happened,' she said.

Mark stared at her for a long time.

'I'll find out.'

He looked out the window. Far away, halfway to Inchmick-ery island, he could see the coastguard speedboat. He tried to remember it from two days ago, when he was taking pictures, when he thought his life was worth living. He couldn't.

It was back out there which meant the pod of whales wasn't in the clear yet either. Good, he wanted them to suffer like he and Ruth were suffering.

He turned to her. He wanted to gouge his own eyes out when he saw the look on her face. He thought about it from her point of view. First her husband missing, then dead, then revealed to have been abusing their daughter. Now this. At least he still had Nathan. His stomach tightened at the thought of the boy.

'What did you do?' he said.

'What?'

Mark stuck a finger in his coffee and wished it was boiling hot.

'I was just wondering what you did, when William first disappeared. Did you try to find out what happened?'

She took a sip of tea. Mark caught a whiff of straw and mint from her mug. Sickly. She nodded.

'What did you do?'

Ruth put her mug down carefully. 'A lot of silly things.'

'Like what?'

'I walked around our neighbourhood, handing out flyers and putting up posters. Went round people's houses until everyone was sick of me. Then, when they found his car at the golf club, I pestered everyone there.'

'And?'

'Then I hired a private detective. Three months of time and money wasted, he came up with nothing either. None of it made me feel any better. At the time I thought at least I was doing something, but really I was just driving myself insane.'

'I already feel insane.'

Mark looked at her and she glanced away.

At the next table, a little girl aged about three was smacking a Peppa Pig bracelet off the table. Clank, clank, clank. Mark remembered Nathan at that age, obsessed with Spiderman. When he was first toilet trained, he and his friends at nursery had been inordinately proud of their Spiderman pants, showing them off to each other and the staff at every possible opportunity. Who would remember that except for Mark, now that Lauren was dead? He was the only one left to tell his family's story, all the stupid, irrelevant stuff that made up who Nathan was, how they related to each other.

The girl was still smacking away. Mark worried that she was going to break the bracelet, and felt like reaching over to stop her. He raised his hand and stared at it as if it was an alien artefact. Rubbed at his fingers with his other hand. The pinkie was cold and stiff, it had been ever since he broke it a few years ago playing football and it was badly reset. Only he and Lauren knew about that. Only him now.

Mark turned to Ruth. 'How am I supposed to tell Nathan?'

Ruth looked as if she was going to take his hand, then had second thoughts.

'I don't know.'

'I can't do it. I can't bear it.'

'Children are amazingly resilient.'

'It's not him I'm worried about.'

This time he felt Ruth's hand on his. He looked at it. Liver spots on slack skin. Her hand was motherly compared to that police officer's, compared to Lauren's. Thicker fingers, wedding and engagement rings tight on her swollen knuckles. He wondered why she still wore them, how she could. As if any of that meant anything.

The espresso machine screamed and hissed, drowning out the noise of mums and kids all around them. He looked at the little girl. She had stopped banging the bracelet and was staring at him. Lauren had been carrying a baby girl. A baby girl who would never meet her parents or her brother, who would never know what it was like to play in a play park or eat ice cream or go on a scooter or watch *Peppa Pig*.

The girl turned to her mum.

'Mummy, that man is staring at me.'

It was only then Mark realised he was crying. He turned away and looked out the window at the implacable spread of water. He felt Ruth squeeze his hand and he wished that touch was Lauren's.

21

Ruth had offered to come with him but he insisted on picking up Nathan alone. He was at the school gates in plenty of time, hands shoved into pockets, face set grim against the strengthening sea breeze. It felt like he was in a daydream, disconnected from the real world.

He could hear the prattle of mums waiting nearby. Usual crap. One was moaning about something the teacher had said about her boy, and she was being backed up by the others. Any tiny slight on the abilities of their little darling prodigies met with scorn and derision. The mums all hated Miss Kennedy, resented her youth and good looks, her easy way with the children, her ability to let all the six-year-old bullshit slide off her when the bell went.

Mark despised them for their puerile complaints. What the hell did they have to be angry about? Badly attended coffee mornings and misplaced uniforms, remedial reading practice and whatever other pointless shit they loved to bitch about all day.

The bell went, that sound producing a Pavlovian response in all the parents from somewhere deep in their brains. Everyone straightened up a little in preparation for the onslaught of mayhem about to be unleashed on the playground.

Miss Kennedy's door opened and kids poured out. Mark

knew all their names, had made a point of learning them all at the beginning of P1 just to show he could, and to keep a handle on Nathan's ever-receding world. So here was Ahmed and Ethan, then Amy and Emily. He knew the ones he liked and the ones he didn't. There was a handful of bampot boys who he'd regularly see kicking other kids or even their parents, others who could throw themselves on the ground in a tantrum worthy of a toddler. He hated them, but right now he also envied their uncontained fury at the world.

Eventually he saw Nathan trudging out. Mark's heart was squeezed as he pictured himself telling the boy about his mum. No one should ever have to go through that, the telling or the hearing. Nobody deserved it. Though life wasn't about what you deserved, he knew that now.

He began walking towards the boy, gliding through the melee around him.

A boy came out the classroom behind Nathan and shoved him hard in the back. Not an accident, not a clumsy mistake from a boy who hadn't found his space in the world yet. A deliberate push. It was Lee, the worst of the bullies, the one who acted like he was entitled to the world.

Nathan stumbled forward and lost his footing. Mark was still fifty yards away. The noise around him seemed deafening. He watched as Nathan righted himself and turned to Lee. Lee had his hair gelled into a spike. Nathan shoved him in the chest. Lee was bigger, sturdier, taller. He snarled at Nathan and punched him hard on the shoulder. Mark was walking, getting closer, but he felt like he was drifting through a nightmare, unable to intervene or interact. Even from this distance the punch to Nathan's shoulder looked sore. Mark felt a twinge of pride when Nathan hardly flinched, instead swinging his schoolbag round to connect with Lee's cheek. The bag looked like it had nothing in it, more of a scuff on Lee's face than anything.

Lee grabbed Nathan's hair and pulled downwards so that Nathan had to lower his head in a movement of subservience. Lee then kicked him hard on the shin, making Nathan pull away hopping, leaving behind a tuft of hair in Lee's hand that Mark could see even from twenty-five yards.

He glanced round briefly to see if Lee's mum was anywhere, but he couldn't spot her. Just a maelstrom of little bobbing heads and gossiping women. He turned back.

The boys were wrestling now, holding each other by the front of their jackets, kicking and trying to lever punches in wherever they could. Nathan was holding his own, despite giving away a big size and reach advantage. Mark had never seen him fight like this before, he was never normally a physical child at all.

He was close to them now as the boys tussled backwards and forwards. He looked beyond them to Miss Kennedy's door, but he couldn't see the teacher anywhere. Where was everyone? What the hell had happened to discipline?

He was nearly there now, as Nathan flattened a heavy hand against the other boy's ear. Lee responded by punching Nathan in the kidneys and then, just as Mark reached the pair of them, his arms outstretched, Lee spat, a large splatter of phlegm hitting Nathan's face and the sleeve of Mark's jacket.

Mark grabbed Lee's collar, hauling him away from Nathan so roughly that Lee was lifted off his feet.

'Get off,' Lee said.

'Stay away from Nathan,' Mark shouted in Lee's face. He

could see tears forming in the boy's eyes, but he didn't know if they were from the exertion, pain, regret, the stupid fucking wind, whatever. He didn't give a shit. For a moment, he just wanted to destroy this boy, make him pay for everything he'd done, for everything that had happened.

'Daddy.' It was Nathan at his side. He felt a tug on his arm, a familiar weight. He ignored it and held tight to Lee's collar.

'Get the fuck off me,' Lee said.

Primary two and he already knew 'fuck'. Mark screwed his fist tight and pulled Lee close to his own face. He looked at his other sleeve, brought it round and wiped the spit from it across Lee's face. Lee squirmed, taken aback by the move.

'I said, leave Nathan alone.'

'You're not my dad. Let me go.'

'How would you like it if I spat in your face?'

'What the hell do you think you're doing?'

A sharp voice, angry, bitter.

Lee's mum appeared from behind Mark and hauled the boy away so that Mark's grip on his jacket was lost. Mark's fist remained where it was, grasping the air.

'How dare you threaten my son,' the woman said. Mark could see the family resemblance, narrow eyes, heavy brow, defiant stare. He wondered for a moment if he and Nathan looked as much alike.

'He hit my son,' Mark said.

'Your boy started it.'

Your boy. Did she even know Nathan's name? Mark knew Lee's name, knew everything about him, could tell from looking at him that he would grow up to be a grabbing, manipulative prick like his mum.

'He's got a name,' Mark said.

The woman was confused for a second. 'What?'

'My son has a name. Please use it.'

This threw her off guard, but she pulled Lee close to her hip. 'I don't care what his name is, he's a thug and a bully.'

Mark felt a colossal weight bearing down on his neck and back, like he was shouldering the whole world. A silence seemed to fall all around him, like a sudden fog, dampening the edges of his vision. Through the smear of the world he saw his fist pull back then drive into the woman's face, square on to her nose, which made a satisfying crunch under his knuckle, sending shivers of joy up his arm and into his brain like an adrenalin shot. His mind fizzed with energy, with possibilities, like a whole new universe had opened up to him and only he could see it, only he was able to explore its infinite depths.

The woman's hand was at her nose now. Drops of blood, surprisingly bright, trickled between her fingers and fell on to the concrete. Her eyes were wide and wet as she stared at Mark.

'You're a fucking maniac,' she shouted, her voice wavering. 'I'm going to have you done for assault.'

Mark was pulled back to reality as the playground swam into focus. Saturated colours, those glaring red uniforms everywhere, mirroring the drips of blood on the ground. And the noise, like sitting under a jet engine, a blasting roar of nothingness.

He turned to Nathan, who was gaping at him with a look Mark had never seen before. He didn't know what it meant, had no idea what was going through the boy's mind, and it struck him that it was just about the first time that was true.

He grabbed Nathan's hand and turned back to Lee and his

mum. He leaned towards the woman, and she cowered despite trying to puff herself up.

'Do what the hell you like,' he said quietly. 'We're going home.'

He walked at a calm clip, Nathan scurrying to keep up. He passed through the playground, other parents turning away from his gaze, their children, beautiful, honest kids, gawping straight at him in shock. He felt like something out of the Bible, a righteous man in a sea of compromise and corruption.

22

Neither of them spoke all the way home. Mark trudged on, his brain mush. How many hundreds of times had they walked up and down this fucking prom? How many more times would they? He couldn't imagine. Before and after, everything now was split into before and after.

As they turned up Marlborough Street Mark slowed down. Instead of pulling at Nathan's hand it was the other way around, Nathan taking the lead. Mark knew what he was doing. Putting it off. If they never reached the flat, never opened the front door, never went inside, then he'd never have to tell Nathan. Maybe they could just stay here in the street forever.

They reached number 12. Mark fumbled in his pockets for the keys, but Nathan just pushed at the door and it opened. Mark thought about that. Sometimes when it was windy the bottom door didn't catch, and Mr Morrison upstairs was always leaving it open. But still.

He remembered as they climbed the stairs that he still hadn't got the door to their flat fixed. Too much other shit, always too much other shit. The door was pulled closed, but that didn't mean anything. He wondered.

'Wait here.' He ushered Nathan into the side of the stairwell.

He eased the door open and waited. Couldn't hear anything. He pushed it further and poked his head round.

'Daddy,' Nathan whispered. Mark glanced back. Nathan had a look on his face that was part scared, part amused. Maybe he thought it was one of Daddy's silly games, like shooting the bins. Maybe this was another *Star Wars* thing.

Mark put his finger to his lips and crept inside.

He went from room to room, his pulse a monstrous thud in his ears.

Nothing. No one around and no sign of a break-in, although it was impossible to tell with the door broken.

He opened the door fully and waved Nathan in.

'What were you doing, Daddy?'

'Just checking something.'

'Is Mummy home?'

Mark closed his eyes. Pictured the dry skin of her lips. Jesus, he wanted a drink. Something to take the edge off this. But he couldn't do it like that. He looked away from the boy.

'No, she's not home.'

'I thought you said she was only going to be away for a couple of days?'

Mark tried to speak but nothing came out.

'Can I play my DS?'

Mark pushed at the bridge of his nose, digging his nails in, pinching the skin, screwing his eyes up until he saw sparks flash on his eyelids.

'Nathan, come here.'

He put an arm out and the boy came and cuddled him. He crouched down and held him right there in the hall until he felt the boy squirm and try to pull away.

'I have to tell you something. And you have to be a big, brave boy, OK?'

Nathan looked worried.

'Promise?'

The boy nodded, just a flick of the head, nothing more.

Mark's eyes were already blurry.

'The thing is, Mummy's not coming back to us.'

Nathan angled his head. 'Are you getting divorced, like Findlay's mum and dad?'

Mark felt his hands shake, tasted the salt of tears on his lips.

'No, we're not getting divorced. She's dead. Mummy's dead.'

The boy's face was blank. He didn't get it. He frowned.

Mark had his hands on the boy's shoulders. 'Do you understand what that means?'

He nodded. 'She's not alive any more. We won't ever see her again.'

'That's right, I'm afraid not.'

Mark's legs buckled and he slumped on to the floor next to the boy. He felt a hand pat his shoulder.

'It's OK, Daddy, don't be upset.'

Mark put his trembling hand on top of the boy's.

'I don't think you understand,' he said.

'Is she in heaven?'

He should just say yes, but even now, in this hole, he couldn't bring himself.

'Some people think so.'

'Do you think so?'

Mark was sobbing, his whole body shaking.

'She's in our hearts,' he said.

Nathan was cuddling him now, and he felt a change in the boy as they clung to each other. Nathan's breath caught a little, then he began sniffling, then full crying. Either he'd finally got it or he was mimicking his dad. For some reason Mark was grateful, this was easier than dealing with a blank-faced boy. But he felt guilty too, as if Nathan's state of mind wasn't proper grief unless it mirrored Mark's own reaction.

All this going on underneath the surface, a sea of self-aware second-guessing.

Nathan was wailing now, a keening noise that wasn't human. Mark gripped him tighter, feeling the sharp edges through his clothes, the brittle delicacy of his bones. He was consumed with guilt and shame at having to do this. Anger too at Lauren for putting him in this position, for somehow not caring enough about life to keep on living it.

They sat like that in the hall for a long time, just holding on to each other.

Eventually the crying began to subside and Mark felt an emptiness sweep over him, a numbing lack of life.

He reached into his pocket and took out a tissue. Pulled back from Nathan a little and began wiping his nose and eyes. The boy's face was a mess, crumpled and red, blood close to the skin. His lower jaw was shaking, like he'd just come out of a freezing bath.

Mark used the same tissue on his own tears and snot, his breath still tripping in irregular hiccups. He swallowed and shook his head.

Nathan's breath was almost back to normal. He looked at Mark.

'How did she die?' His voice was higher than usual, and it snagged on the last word.

Mark should've looked this up on the fucking internet. What was the correct way of doing this? What was the correct response to expect from a kid? Nothing he could think of seemed to fit or make sense any more.

'Never mind about that just now.'

'Daddy, how did she die?' There was a steeliness in the boy's voice.

Mark stared at his son. 'She drowned in the sea.'

'Was it sore?'

Mark rubbed at his eyes, took big gulps of air. 'No, it wasn't sore.'

'Why didn't she swim?'

'What?'

'If she was in the sea, why didn't she just swim back to shore?'

'It's not as simple as that.'

'Why not? Mummy's a good swimmer.'

'Yes, I know she is, but . . .'

'Why was she in the sea anyway? It's freezing.'

'They don't know why she was in the sea.'

'Who are they?'

'The police.'

'Why are the police interested?'

'It's their job to find out how people die.'

'Is that what they're doing now? Trying to find out?'

Mark thought about that. Pictured a post-mortem. Easy enough, he'd seen hundreds of fake ones on television. He felt his stomach lurch as he saw someone cutting down the middle of her chest.

'Yes, they're trying to find out.'

'Maybe it was an accident. Maybe she slipped and fell in.'

Jesus.

'Maybe.'

'Or maybe someone pushed her in.'

'Don't think about it just now, Nathan.'

The boy's face hardened and his eyes went wide.

'Maybe you pushed her in, Daddy.'

'What?'

'Maybe she tried to leave us again, like last time, when I was born, and you stopped her by pushing her in the sea.'

Mark had his hands on Nathan's shoulders. The boy was crying again.

'Why would she want to leave us?' Nathan was full-on sobbing.

'She didn't want to leave us, OK?'

'She did,' Nathan said. 'She already left us before. That first time. When I was a baby.'

'That was years ago.'

'Was it because of me?'

'What?'

'Was it because she didn't want to have me?'

Mark pulled Nathan into a bear hug. 'Christ, it's nothing like that. It's complicated, grown-up stuff. She loved you so much, though, you have to understand that.'

Nathan could hardly speak through the crying. 'Then why is she dead? Why isn't she still here?'

And there it was, the end point.

Why wasn't she still here.

The giant lump of stone in his gut.

Why.

'I don't know. I don't know.'

They were back to sobbing again, the pair of them in the hall, holding on as if the floor might give way underneath.

Mark stroked the boy's hair until eventually the crying had reduced to a sniffle. Wiped Nathan's face again, then his own, the tissue now a torn, damp rag.

He tried to think of something normal to say or do, but nothing seemed normal. He couldn't stand any more of this raw emotion, couldn't bear to look in Nathan's eyes and see the understanding, the desolation, or whatever was in there.

'Why don't we put on *Star Wars*,' he said, shocked at the words as he spoke them. 'You can watch a bit while I make something to eat.'

Was it even time for a meal? Mark had no ability to tell if he was hungry or not, the link from his body to his brain seemed to be severed.

Nathan gave a slight nod of the head as he wiped at his eyes with his sleeves.

'Which film do you want to watch?' Mark said.

This was really happening, then. Life was apparently going on without her.

Nathan shook his head. It was the first time ever he hadn't had a preference.

Mark found himself racing through the films in his head. Luke's aunt and uncle killed and burned in the original film, all that dark shit in *The Empire Strikes Back*, Padmé dying in childbirth at the end of *Revenge of the Sith*. Shit. Anakin leaving his mum for ever in *The Phantom Menace*. Fuck fuck fuck.

He pushed himself up against the wall and took Nathan's hand.

'Come on, I'll choose.'

And they walked through to the living room as if they were a normal father and son.

23

The stomach cramps started around half seven, just as Nathan was getting ready for bed.

Mark was trying to keep things as normal as possible, sticking to the routine. Nathan had already asked if he could sleep in Mummy and Daddy's bed, and Mark agreed straight away, thinking maybe they'd each draw some comfort from it. Either that or it would just remind them of what had happened.

He was churning it all over in his mind, trying to organise his thoughts. A death is either an accident, suicide or murder. So what about Lauren? If it was an accident, how the hell did it happen? You don't just accidentally fall into the sea, not around here, that didn't make any sense. If it was murder, the big questions were who and why? Why would anyone want to murder Lauren? Unless it was just a random mugging or something that went wrong. But then how did her body end up in the sea? Mark tried to remember her body lying on the beach, but his mind skipped past it. Had there been any signs of murder? He couldn't think of any, but that didn't mean anything.

So that left suicide. Had she killed herself? And the unborn child? That was the most unbearable thing of all. He knew about depression from the time before, how it was an illness, and the person suffering from it wasn't themselves and all that excusing bullshit. But at the end of all that, suicide was cowardly, it was desertion. He could understand how she could leave him behind, he was just her husband, just a man she maybe loved. But Nathan? And the second kid? How could she just give up on them like that? It was unthinkable.

Nathan came through from putting his jammies on with a sour look on his face.

'I've got a sore tummy, Daddy.'

It was a familiar whine, not a real complaint, a little whimper for attention.

Mark held out his hand and Nathan came over and sat on his lap. Too big for that but what the hell.

'Show me where.'

Nathan pointed to the side of his stomach and Mark rubbed gently at his abdomen. It felt tight.

'When did you last go for a poo?'

Nathan shrugged. They'd been through this once before, constipation. They'd bought some sickly-sweet medicine over the counter which had eventually done the trick, a torrent of shit pouring out behind a hard plug twelve hours later. He didn't want to go through that again.

'I'll give you some of that tummy medicine, OK?'

He felt the boy's muscles tense under his hand.

'Ow, it really hurts.'

It seemed like more than just a moan now, maybe some real pain.

'And some Calpol too.'

Mark went to the bathroom and came back with the two bottles.

Nathan was watching some crap on the telly, a bloopers show. He winced and reached for his side.

Mark gave him the maximum amount of each medicine. If nothing else, the Calpol might help him sleep.

'Hopefully that'll stop it hurting.'

Nathan kept his eyes on the screen.

'Daddy, is Mummy going to be buried or burned?'

Shit, Mark hadn't even got that far yet. Lauren had wanted cremation, better for the environment. He was going to have to sort all that out. More weight pressing down on him.

He sat down next to the boy.

'She wanted to be cremated, that means burned.'

'At a funeral?'

'That's right.'

'Do I have to be there?'

Mark looked at his son and felt like screaming.

'You don't have to, but you can if you want. It's up to you.'

'I'd like to come,' Nathan said. 'When is it?'

'I don't know.' Mark thought about the post-mortem, Lauren cold in the morgue. 'Soon, I suppose.'

'OK.'

At least it had taken his mind off the stomach cramps.

'Time for bed,' Mark said, getting up.

Nathan reached for the remote and switched the television off. No moaning, no playing for extra time. Mark watched every one of his son's movements as if he was an exotic animal at the zoo, a panther pacing in its cage.

He got the boy into bed. Read *Too Many Daves*, something light and stupid, no moral stuff tonight, just silly wordplay. Then Mark lay there on the bed next to Nathan, stroking the boy's head until his breathing slowed and steadied, and his body slackened into sleep.

Mark must've fallen asleep himself, because he was jolted out of it by crying and moaning.

Nathan next to him, clutching at his side and his stomach, tears already on his cheeks.

'It hurts, Daddy.'

'Shhh, it's OK.' Mark rubbed the boy's belly. It felt hard, distended maybe. Jesus.

Mark checked the time. Back of eight. They'd only been asleep for a few minutes.

Nathan was ramping it up. Wails and cries of pain now, writhing under the covers, grabbing at his own body as if possessed, consumed by something.

Mark tried to talk over the noise, tried to keep his voice steady.

'Show me where it hurts.'

Nathan pointed to the left-hand side of his stomach. Was that where the appendix was? Nathan was screaming now, floods of tears. Unbearable.

Mark held him, the boy's body in spasms as he tried to wriggle free from the pain.

After a few minutes it seemed to ebb away, then moments later it came back. Waves of crying and squirming and clutching. Mark had never seen him like this before.

'Sod it,' he said. 'Let's go to Sick Kids.'

Being forced into action seemed to calm Nathan down. Focusing on something other than the cramps. Mark got their shoes and jackets on, Nathan still in his jammies underneath. He grabbed the car key and Nathan's DS, anything to distract him on the way and in the A&E waiting room.

They shuffled out the door, downstairs and into the car.

Mark tried to put the boy's seatbelt on but he screamed in pain, another wave of agony.

'OK,' Mark said. 'Take it easy.'

He drove across town, the city bathed in evening light, diffuse springtime. The wind had died. Around Cameron Toll, one lane was closed because of a fallen tree, council workmen standing around with a chainsaw scratching their heads.

Nathan went from screams to crying snuffles as the pain came and went.

They got to Sick Kids A&E, an anonymous door down a side road round from the red-brick front of the main hospital. Mark carried the boy inside. At the reception, Nathan was hit by another stab of pain, shouting and crying and doubling up in Mark's arms.

They jumped the queue as a result, straight into a treatment room where a mid-twenties female doctor in a tight Hello Kitty T-shirt began prodding at Nathan's belly.

Nathan whimpered as she moved her hands, but the pain seemed to have receded. Mark wanted to explain that he'd been screaming and writhing in agony minutes before, but he couldn't think of a way of saying it that didn't sound pathetic. So he just sat there, useless, as the woman pushed her fingers into Nathan's abdomen.

A television was on in the corner of the room playing a DVD. Some *Ben 10* thing. Nathan would've been mesmerised eighteen months ago. Strange how quickly these obsessions came and went.

The doctor asked Nathan a few questions and he answered dutifully. She gave Mark a look which he couldn't decipher.

What the fuck are you doing wasting my time, maybe. Or, have you been abusing this poor wee kid?

She turned to Nathan.

'I'm just going to have a word with your dad outside, OK, Nathan?'

The boy nodded. The pain seemed to have gone now. Mark felt ridiculous.

Outside, the woman gave him a smile suitable for toddlers. She was pretty and young, firm-skinned and confident.

'It's most likely constipation or something similar,' she said.

'Sorry.'

She shook her head. 'Not at all, we get some extremely distressing cases of constipation in here. In all honesty, I don't know what's causing it.'

'He was in a lot of pain before.' Mark hated the sound of his own voice.

'I'm sure he was. The truth is we never find out the root cause in half of all stomach complaints in children. There's an outside chance it's his appendix. The pain is on the opposite side, but sometimes appendicitis does present on the left.'

Mark stood looking at the doctor's T-shirt. Maybe their second child, their daughter, would've been into Hello Kitty as much as Nathan was into *Star Wars*.

'His mum just died,' Mark said.

'I beg your pardon?'

Mark rubbed his forehead. 'My wife, Nathan's mum. She was found dead today on Portobello beach.'

'Oh my God, I'm so sorry.' There was genuine concern in her voice, whatever that was worth.

'I just told him this evening. Could that have something to do with this?'

The look on the girl's face made Mark turn away from her.

'Maybe,' she said. 'Pain is a very complex thing, especially in children. They quite often don't differentiate between physical and mental pain.'

'You mean it could be psychosomatic.'

'That's not really how we put it.'

'How would you put it?'

Mark felt a touch on his sleeve.

'The important thing is that he seems OK now,' the doctor said. 'The best thing you can do is be there for him.'

'That's it?'

'Mr Douglas, I'm not a counsellor, I'm a doctor.'

Mark just stood there like a dead tree in a storm.

'Look, in cases like this, we sometimes keep the child in hospital overnight, just to keep an eye on them. It almost never turns out to be appendicitis. But I think in this instance, Nathan and you would prefer to be at home, wouldn't you? In more familiar surroundings. Given what's happened.'

Mark nodded. It felt like a completely involuntary movement.

'We can give him some more laxative, pain relief and perhaps a small sedative,' the doctor said. 'If there's any reoccurrence of the symptoms, don't hesitate to come back in.'

Mark couldn't speak, as if his brain had given up and shut down. He could hear *Ben 10* playing inside the room. No noise coming from Nathan.

He opened the door. The boy was half-asleep, head lolled over to the side.

'I'll get that medication for you,' the doctor said.

Mark climbed up on to the treatment table, not really enough room for him but he squeezed in.

'How's the tummy now, Big Guy?'

'Fine.'

On screen, Ben as Upchuck was vomiting some kind of toxic bile all over his enemies and saving the day. Then he changed into XLR8 and sped away from all the baddies.

The doctor came back with medicine bottles Mark had to sign for, then they trudged through reception, past a worried mum holding a bloody tea towel to her three-year-old daughter's eye.

Mark unlocked the car and Nathan clambered in.

'Daddy?'

'What?'

Nathan was holding something in his hand. In the darkness of the car, Mark couldn't make it out.

'What is it?'

'My other tooth.'

Mark put his hand out and Nathan dropped it in. Another tiny gem, a little part of Nathan that he was never going to get back. Mark wondered if he had another two-pound coin.

'How did that happen?'

Nathan shrugged. 'It just came out, that's all.'

'Do you want me to look after it on the way home?'

Nathan shook his head. 'I'll hold it, Daddy. That way it will be safe.'

Mark handed the tooth back and strapped the boy in. He thought about when the first tooth came out, how Nathan was so keen to tell Mummy about it.

On the drive home Nathan fell asleep with the motion of the car, still clutching the baby tooth tightly in his fist.

Mark remembered the first ever drive with him, back home from the hospital the day after he was born, Lauren in the passenger seat, both of them exhausted, but also ecstatic, fretful, overawed by the whole thing. They were allowed to take this tiny human home with them. They were being entrusted with his care. Feeding him and keeping him clean and changing his nappies and burping him and trying to work out what the hell was the matter at three in the morning when he was crying and crying and they had no clue.

From there, he had another flash of memory. In a hire car, him and Lauren parked on a shoreline somewhere north of Ullapool, looking at a stupendous sunset, the sun taking forever to drop below the horizon, leaving smudges of purple and orange streaking across the sky. They sat waiting to see the northern lights – the old lady at their cheap B&B had said atmospheric conditions were just right at the moment. But they never came, those magical lights in the sky, that would've been too perfect.

They didn't mind, sitting there joking, listening to Teenage Fanclub, their lives spread out in the sky ahead of them, talking about all that clichéd crap that couples do in the mess of love. They kissed then clambered into the back seat, moving quickly, pulling at each other's clothes, Lauren climbing on top of him and pushing down, Mark clutching her hips to push himself in deeper. They both came quickly and laughed, looking around nervously to see if anyone had seen them.

They didn't know for sure if that was when Nathan was conceived, but the dates were close. They were at it like rabbits that holiday, having decided to try for a baby, so it could've been any one of a dozen times. In a perfect world they would've seen the northern lights fizzle across the expanse of sky. Instead, they just fumbled their clothes back on and wiped down the back seat of the hire car before climbing out and going for a walk along the beach, arm in arm, content with their simple lives.

24

He was swimming with fellow pilot whales, amazed at the fluency of his movements as he ducked in and out of the pod, Lauren and Nathan alongside him, whales as well. They were contented at first, then the mood of the pod changed, panic setting in as the water got more shallow. A speedboat's propellers cut the surface of the sea above them as the waves and wind pushed them closer to land, all of them frenzied and thrashing, colliding and squirming over and under each other. He felt rough sand on his belly as he was pushed on to the beach, Lauren and Nathan following him. He tried to tell them not to follow him on to land where they would get stranded, but he couldn't speak. They nudged on in his wake, trusting him to look after them as he betrayed them and led them to their deaths on the sand.

He was woken by a noise. Knocking at the door. He looked round. Light streaming through the gap in the curtains, Nathan sprawled diagonally across the double bed, still asleep. The clock said 10.15 a.m. Too late for school, even if that had been an option. There were three empty beer bottles by the bed.

He'd stayed up till the early hours on his phone, Googling post-mortem procedures and children's reactions to grief, scanning the Caledonia Dreaming website, Lauren's Facebook and Twitter pages. Scanned back and forward through all the pictures she was tagged in, touching the screen and crying. Self-aware but also somehow oblivious to it all, wallowing in misery.

The knocking noise again. They should've been downstairs using the buzzer if the bottom door was closed.

He got up. He hadn't undressed last night. He padded to the door and looked through the fish-eye spy hole. Ferguson and a man, an overweight, middle-aged, no-bullshit guy, by the look of him.

Mark opened the door.

'Mr Douglas,' Ferguson said. It had been Mark yesterday, not Mr Douglas. Something had changed. 'Can we come in?'

Mark sighed, then opened the door further. The two of them bustled into the hall, struggling to turn round in the cramped space.

'This is Detective Inspector Green,' Ferguson said. The man offered his hand. He had an air of authority, he was clearly Ferguson's boss.

Mark stared at them both. 'Well?'

'We've got the result of your wife's post-mortem,' Ferguson said.

Mark had a roaring noise in his ears and struggled to hear her. He felt an intense heat sweep over his body, making him flush.

'And?'

'Lauren was murdered, Mr Douglas.'

He reached out and leaned against the wall. It felt as if the floor was tilting away from him, like he was on a boat in heavy seas.

Ferguson looked down. 'There was evidence of strangulation.

She was dead before she went in the water. She definitely didn't drown.'

Mark's vision was out of focus. He pictured her on the beach, the smell of salt water, the cracked blue lips. Tried to think about her neck. Strangled. Pain and fear and terror. Not a peaceful death at all. Was it sore, Daddy? The last thing she would've seen was her killer, the image burnt on to her retinas until the end of time. He squeezed his eyes shut.

'We need to speak to you down at the station,' Green said.

'What?'

'This is a murder inquiry now, Mr Douglas.'

He blinked. 'And you think I killed her.'

At least Ferguson had the decency to look away from him. 'No, but you were one of the last people to see her, so we need to take you in for a formal interview, that's all.'

'Daddy?'

Nathan stood at the doorway of the bedroom, rubbing his eyes. Mark went to him.

'How's your tummy, Big Guy?'

'It's fine.' Nathan smiled, held something up. 'Look.'

It was another two-pound coin.

'The tooth fairy came again. How cool is that?'

'Very cool.'

Nathan looked past him. 'Who are these people? Is something wrong?'

'Nothing's wrong.'

'Is it about Mummy?'

'Don't worry about it,' Mark said. 'Why don't you go through and put the telly on, I'll make some toast.'

'Am I not going to school today?'

Mark shook his head. 'Don't worry about school. You're having a day off. Now go watch telly for a bit.'

Nathan shuffled his feet. 'I think I need a poo.'

'That's good. Go sit on the toilet then.'

The extractor fan whirred into life as Nathan turned the light on in the bathroom. He sat on the toilet clutching his tooth-fairy money. He didn't close the door. No one in their family ever closed the door, but then they never had the police hanging around in their hall before.

Mark turned to Ferguson. 'What am I supposed to do with him?'

'Either bring him to the station and we can have a social worker sit with him, or maybe there's someone else you could call to come round and watch him?'

He didn't want Nathan at the station.

'Daddy, I'm doing a poo,' Nathan hollered from the toilet.

'That's great,' Mark shouted back. He turned to the police. 'We were up at Sick Kids last night. Stomach cramps. The doctor reckoned it was most likely constipation.'

'There's loads of poo,' Nathan said.

Mark looked at Ferguson and Green. 'Let me just make a phone call.'

25

The interview room wasn't like those concrete shit-holes you saw on television, two-way mirror on one side and no windows. This was more like a pod in a call centre, with a scratchy brown carpet, metal and fabric chairs, a phone and an ancient computer on a desk. There was even a window, looking out over the flats round the back of the station. Somewhere beyond those buildings, the pilot whales were flipping and slapping through the waves.

He thought about Nathan. Ruth had answered her phone on the first ring. He then spent an excruciating half-hour waiting for her to come round, Ferguson and Green lurking in the kitchen while he sat with Nathan watching a crappy *Clone Wars* cartoon, the boy transfixed on Ahsoka and Anakin slicing their way through a million battle droids.

Mark got changed into fresh clothes in the bedroom, aware of the cops at the other end of the flat, probably going through the kitchen cupboards for clues. He slid the wardrobe drawer open and darted a hand in. Pistol still there. He finished dressing and went back to Nathan, wondering if he would ever get the chance to sit on the sofa watching this shit with the boy again.

So now he was in a police interview room, waiting. He could see two gulls scrapping over something on a rooftop across the road. He could hear shrieks and the skitter of their feet on the tiles. The station was silent. Easy life being a cop, obviously.

He stuck his hand in his pocket and felt Nathan's two milk teeth in there. Pulled them out and examined them. Rubbed at them with his thumb, felt the smoothness of the enamel against his skin. He wondered about making a wish, but then the door opened. He slid the teeth back into his pocket.

Ferguson and Green sat down across the desk from him. Mark noticed more crime-prevention posters on the walls. Was there a never-ending supply of these things? Shouldn't they be spending money on actually preventing crimes, rather than making endless posters about it?

Ferguson looked apologetic. She pulled a digital recorder out, laid it on the desk and switched it on. Mark looked at it, red light blinking.

'Do I need my lawyer for this?'

'Do you have a lawyer?'

'No.'

She shook her head. 'You're not under caution.'

Mark sat upright in his seat. 'So I could just get up and leave?'

'If you like. But I thought you might want to help us find the person who killed your wife.'

Mark scratched at his neck. 'Shit.'

Ferguson's face seemed to soften. Green shifted his bulk, stared at Mark. It looked as if the chair was struggling to hold together under his weight.

'I realise this is hard for you,' Ferguson said.

Had she said that before? She had no fucking clue.

'Let's just get this over with,' Mark said. 'So I can get back to Nathan.'

Ferguson looked at him. 'Yes, about that.'

'What?'

'That was Lauren's mother who came round to look after him, correct?'

'Yes.'

'Ruth Bell?'

Mark frowned. 'Yes.'

'The same Ruth Bell who has a restraining order out against you since an incident five years ago?'

Mark raised a hand. 'Now wait a minute.'

'We're not complete idiots, Mr Douglas, we do check people's police records.'

'That was all a misunderstanding.'

'You'd be amazed how often we hear that from violent people.'

'I'm not a violent person.'

'And yet your mother-in-law has a restraining order out against you after a violent assault that occurred on her property.'

'That was a long time ago, it's all been sorted.'

'Would you like to tell us what it was about?'

'Not really.'

'That's hardly doing your cause any good.'

Mark sighed. 'Lauren was sexually abused by her dad as a kid. It came out in counselling. Ruth didn't believe her. Things got heated, that's all.'

'This would be William Bell, who was found dead seven years ago?'

Mark stared at her. 'That has got nothing to do with Lauren's death.'

Ferguson shuffled some papers and glanced at DI Green. 'We've looked at the file on Mr Bell's death and there's no mention of child abuse.'

Mark rubbed at his temple. 'That's because no one knew about it when he went missing.'

Ferguson raised her eyebrows and straightened her mouth. Looking for more.

'Lauren only remembered about it during therapy after her postnatal depression, after she went missing the first time.'

'That's quite convenient.'

'I'm sorry?'

'Lauren was abused by her own father. That's a pretty good motive for doing him some harm. I'm just saying it's handy for her she apparently didn't remember about it at the time of his death.'

'I can't believe you're implying Lauren had anything to do with her dad's death.'

'And what about Mrs Bell?'

'What about her?'

'She didn't know anything about what her husband had done?'

Mark remembered his conversation with Ruth in her house. 'No.'

'Also pretty convenient.'

'Look, you're way off course here,' Mark said.

'And you didn't know anything about the abuse either, when Mr Bell went missing?'

'Of course not.'

'How did you feel?'

'About what?'

'When Lauren told you she'd been sexually abused by her own dad.'

'I felt sick and furious, OK? I was glad the old bastard was dead. Now can we get back to talking about Lauren's murder?'

Ferguson put the papers down on the desk.

'I believe you underwent anger management classes.'

Mark ran a hand through his hair. 'Yes, as part of the court verdict after the thing with Ruth. What about it?'

'How did you find the experience, Mr Douglas?'

'I don't see what this has to do with anything.'

Ferguson looked up at him. 'I'm just trying to get a feel for your domestic situation, that's all.'

'My domestic situation was perfectly fine until someone murdered my wife.'

Ferguson frowned. 'A father-in-law dead in suspicious circumstances, a violent assault on your mother-in-law, and now you're telling me about child sex abuse. It doesn't sound perfectly fine to me.'

'You're twisting things,' Mark said. 'None of that is relevant to Lauren now. If you don't believe me, go and ask Ruth.'

'Don't worry, we'll certainly be talking to Mrs Bell in due course. About a number of things.'

Mark rubbed his hand over his face. Thick stubble. When did he last shave?

'OK,' Ferguson said. 'Tell me about the last time you saw your wife.'

Mark slumped. 'I told you all this when I reported her missing.'

'Tell us again.'

He knew what they were doing. He'd seen enough crime

dramas on television. They were getting the story several times, looking for inconsistencies.

Ferguson put a hand out in front of her, an invitation to speak. 'Please, Mr Douglas.'

Mark had a flash of Lauren, clammy and wet in his arms, the tang of seaweed burning his nostrils. He breathed forcefully out of his mouth.

Ferguson watched him closely. 'The sooner we get this done, the sooner you can get back to your son.' She was using a soft voice, no doubt part of the training. 'Isn't that what you want?'

Mark sighed and turned to the inspector. 'What about you? Don't you speak?'

Green pursed his lips. 'DC Ferguson is perfectly capable of conducting this interview.'

Mark turned back to Ferguson. 'This is bullshit, you should be out finding the person who killed my wife.'

'We will. Now tell me about the last time you saw Lauren.'

Mark went through it all again. Tried to remember. He tried to picture her in bed that morning, or walking through the house with a mug of tea in one hand, a piece of toast in the other. But all he could see was her cracked blue lips, her lank, salty hair in his hands.

The questions kept trundling out. Had they argued recently? What sort of mood was she in that morning? What about before that? How did she feel about being pregnant? Had either of them ever had affairs? How would he describe their relationship? How was she doing at work? Did she have any worries about anything else?

That got Mark thinking about Gavin Taylor. Spending all that time working alongside Lauren at the office. A married man with family now, but what about all the history with Lauren? He used to fancy her, maybe he still did. Maybe it was mutual. He tried to picture Taylor's face when he confronted him at the office. Then again at his house. Did he look guilty? The kind of look someone has when they know something. What the hell did that even look like?

He started talking about Taylor, about the possibility he was involved. Something Mark didn't want to think about, that Taylor and Lauren could've been together. But he had to think about it now.

Ferguson was non-committal. She scribbled occasional notes on a pad, checked the red light on the recorder. Green was crunching on an apple. A fucking apple. Good luck, coronary-boy.

Mark's voice dried up. He reached for a plastic cup of water on the desk and sipped. He was shocked at how cold the water was. He wondered if it was as cold as the sea just beyond those flats out the window, the last place Lauren had been. But she wasn't alive in the water, was she.

Mark screwed his eyes shut and sipped. Water went down the wrong way and he coughed, his breath catching, the gag reflex kicking in, his whole body shaking with spasms until Green heaved out his chair, lumbered across and whacked him on the back to clear his throat.

He got his breath back as Green hovered behind him, arm raised, ready to thump him again. Mark held up a hand to stop him, then rested his elbows on the table and looked at Ferguson.

'Gavin Taylor,' he said, nodding. 'Go and see Gavin Taylor. I think he knows something.'

26

He walked back along the prom. The crazy wind had picked up again and he welcomed the insult of it in his face, relished the resistance to his walking and breathing that it provided. Life was resistance now, just trudging on in the face of it.

The whales were back. He'd lost track of their story, hadn't they made it out the firth and into the North Sea? Fucking morons. There was a camera crew set up on the sand, at least one newspaper reporter and photographer that Mark could see, though he didn't recognise them, must be from a different paper. He thought about the *Standard*. He hadn't answered his phone or emails from them. Probably lost the freelance gig now. Add it to the list of things that had fallen apart. On the beach, a handful of punters were pointing camera phones out to sea. Everyone was a photographer now anyway, his days were numbered.

Fins and snouts were circling and cutting through the wash a hundred yards out. It couldn't be very deep there at all. There were two coastguard boats now, they'd obviously enlisted some help. They were doing a piss-poor job of herding the pilot whales. A couple of guys in waders and waterproofs were standing in the shallows slapping at the water with large tools like snow shovels. Splash, splash. It made sod-all difference to the whales, who were oblivious to the whole thing. If they wanted to kill themselves, why didn't everyone just let them die?

Mark watched the display for a while, mind churning like the waves. He had to find out about Lauren. But he didn't trust the police to do anything. He would have to find out himself. At least the police didn't seem to seriously think he had anything to do with it, despite all that bullshit about the restraining order and the anger management.

Strangled, Jesus.

He raised a trembling hand to his head and leaned against the concrete seawall. Closed his eyes. Felt the wind buffeting him, trying to knock him off balance.

'Excuse me.'

He opened his eyes. A little boy about three was standing on the wall, his mum thirty yards back, struggling to catch up.

'What?' Mark said.

'Can you move, please?'

Mark frowned. The boy looked at Mark's body, slumped on the wall.

'Sorry?' Mark said.

'Can you move?'

The mum caught up. 'I'm sorry,' she said to Mark, then to the boy: 'Come down, Aidan, stop bothering the man.'

She helped him jump off the wall and held his hand as they walked round Mark, then she lifted him back on to the wall.

Mark suddenly understood what the boy had been asking. Why hadn't he realised at the time? Stupid, stupid. Like he was in a trance.

'Sorry,' he said.

The woman turned a little and looked back.

Mark shouted to her. 'Sorry, I didn't realise.'

The woman made a flustered wave and carried on walking with the boy.

Aidan. Sounded a bit like Nathan. He remembered Nathan at that age, the toilet training, getting him out of his cot and into his first bed. The occasional tantrums, the obsessive phases. He'd levelled off now, a good kid, solid, sensible, sweet-natured. How would all this affect him?

He thought about the unborn baby. He would never have all that stuff again, the sleepless newborn panic, the delirious, frazzled mania of it. He pictured Lauren naked on a slab in the morgue, her body cut open, the embryo nestled inside, sucking her thumb.

He leaned over the wall and puked, thin bile dripping down the concrete and making tiny holes in the sand. He gave himself over to the involuntary spasms, gave up control of his body, drowned himself in the freedom of loss.

People walked past pretending to ignore him. No one stopped. He wouldn't stop either if he was them.

He spat, the wind tugging a string of phlegm from his mouth. He wiped his face with his sleeve. He rubbed at his wet eyes, blinked and looked out to sea. The guys standing in the water were still slapping at the surface, the whales circling near the shore, the speedboats cutting through the waves. The world was just carrying on whether he gave up on it or not.

He turned and headed up Marlborough Street.

Just outside the flat, he saw a young woman coming towards him. She had big eyes and long brown hair, and was carrying a notepad. He didn't recognise her, but he recognised her type from working with plenty of reporters over the years.

'Mr Douglas?'

'I have nothing to say to you.'

'My name is Debbie McAlpine.'

'I don't care what your name is, I'm not talking to you.'

'I'm from the *Daily Record*. I'm so sorry to hear about your wife, Mr Douglas.'

So she was a redtop. Digging deeper, bigger budgets, more hungry for scandal. It didn't bode well that they were already on this.

The woman tucked her hair behind her ear. 'I was just wondering if I could have a reaction from you to the news?'

'No comment.'

'Do you know if the police suspect foul play?'

Mark shook his head.

'I believe you've just come from the police station. What did they say? Were they interviewing you?'

Mark took a step towards her. 'Leave me alone.'

She lowered the notepad. 'It's better for you if you speak to me, Mr Douglas. You don't want to get on the wrong side of the *Daily Record*.'

Mark clenched his fists at his sides. 'It's better for you if you leave me the hell alone.'

'Are you threatening me, Mr Douglas?'

Mark turned from her. 'Just go away.'

He opened the door, went inside and closed it. Leaned against the wall of the stairwell, squeezing his fists and trying to get his breathing back to normal.

27

He heard a familiar tinny sound as he opened the door of the flat, the 'Imperial March' from *Star Wars*. Nathan's DS. He ran his hand over the broken lock, rough splinters sticking out. He snagged one on his finger, flinched, but then pushed his finger on to it until he saw a spot of blood appear.

'How was it?'

Ruth behind him. He sucked at his finger and turned.

'OK.' Mark looked past her to the living room. Nathan was on the sofa, head down, immersed in his fantasy world. Maybe that's how he'd get through all this, live in the *Star Wars* universe till it was safe to come back to reality. 'How have things been here?'

He and Lauren used to have a routine, every day when she came in from work. How was your day, dear? Nice day at the office, dear? Not funny, not a joke, but just a way of saying, amongst it all, that they were still close. They were mocking the emotionally distant husband and wife cliché of seventies sitcoms that they both vaguely remembered.

Ruth turned to look at Nathan. 'Great,' she said. 'We've been having a good time, haven't we, Nathan?'

Nathan paused his DS game and looked up. 'Yeah.'

'Tell Daddy what we've been up to.'

Nathan looked puzzled for a moment. Mark wondered about

his attention span with that bloody console. That horse had bolted long ago, of course. Nathan smiled as he remembered.

'We baked some cakes.'

Mark realised he could smell it. Why hadn't he noticed before, were his senses shutting down on him? The warm waft of baking filled the flat. He couldn't remember ever having that smell in the place before. He and Lauren weren't exactly domestic gods.

'Why don't you go and get them from the kitchen,' Ruth said to Nathan. 'They've probably cooled down by now.'

Nathan shot up and through the house, came back in with a grin and a plate of cupcakes covered in white icing and edible *Star Wars* stickers. Mark picked a Death Star one, Nathan took a Yoda one.

'Can I still play my DS even though you're home, Daddy?'

'Of course.'

The boy flumped back on to the sofa and the Darth Vader theme started up.

'Would you like a cup of something?' Ruth said. Like it was her house.

'I'll get it,' Mark said, staring at the top of Nathan's head, the whorls of hair, the dizzying spread of follicles.

Ruth touched his arm and led him through to the kitchen. She made tea in a teapot. He never usually drank tea, only Lauren did that, and he didn't even know they had a teapot. Where did Ruth find it?

They sat at the dining table, steam from their mugs disappearing into the air between them. Ruth was wearing the same green cardigan she'd had on at her house. Her hair was in a bun. She looked older every time he saw her, or maybe that was just Mark.

'He's a good boy,' she said, nodding down the hall.

'Yeah.'

'He needs you to be strong.'

'I know.' Mark smelled the tea. Thought of Lauren. Thirty years from now, the smell of tea would still remind him of her. Until he died, that's what tea would mean to him.

'I have to find out who did it,' he said.

Ruth tightened her mouth. 'I think you should concentrate on being with Nathan.'

'It's not that simple. I have to know.'

'I understand that, believe me. But sometimes you never find out the truth.'

Mark looked at her. The window behind her cast her features into shadow. The creases around her eyes, the extra flesh at her neck, darkness across her face.

'You mean like with William?'

'I don't think this is the time to talk about that.'

Mark looked at her. 'You know what's strange? In a weird way, it's good knowing that Lauren was murdered. That's a terrible thing to say. But it's true. Just to know what happened, and to know she didn't do it to herself and the baby. You know?'

Ruth breathed in and out shakily. 'I know.'

Mark took a sip of tea. 'The police want to speak to you.'

Ruth looked surprised. 'Really?'

'They asked me about the restraining order.'

'What did you tell them?'

'The truth. That it was a terrible mistake.' He looked out of the window. 'They think I'm a violent person. That I might have done that to Lauren.'

Ruth looked horrified.

'Don't tell me it hadn't crossed your mind as well,' Mark said.

She shook her head. 'It hadn't, Mark. It really hadn't.'

He didn't know if that was the truth, but he was thankful to her for saying it.

'But who could've done such a thing?' she said.

'That's what I aim to find out.'

'Don't do anything dangerous. Grief can make you do the strangest things.'

'I'll be careful.'

'Did the police say when they might release the body for the funeral?'

Mark scrunched his eyes shut then opened them again. He hadn't even asked about that. He imagined someone cutting her body open and looking inside. Imagined another person placing a hand on her neck and squeezing the life out of her.

He shook his head. 'They didn't mention it.'

'Well, if you need any help arranging things, I'm here.' Behind her, the sky outside was cloudy now, a grey wall pummelling across the sky. Trees shook in the wind. Her face was more clearly visible with the sunshine gone. 'And if you need any help looking after Nathan, please phone me.'

'Of course.'

'We need to take care of that wee boy of yours. He's all we have left.'

Mark sat back in his chair but didn't speak. There was nothing else to say. He rubbed at his face. He really needed a shave and a shower.

He heard something from the other room. The *Star Wars* music wasn't playing any more. Instead he heard a wail he recognised.

Mark scraped his chair back and bolted through the flat. In the living room Nathan was sitting on the sofa, knees pulled up to his chin, rocking and crying, thick sobs choking out of him.

Mark held him and shushed him and spoke in a low voice, murmuring comforting words he didn't believe in any more.

'I wish Mummy was here,' Nathan said between gasps, tears soaking his cheeks.

Mark was crying as he gripped the boy's shoulders and held on.

'I know, Big Guy. Me too.'

28

'Have you spoken to Taylor yet?'

'It's not that simple, Mr Douglas.'

Mark was striding in circles around his kitchen, gripping the phone tight. 'It is that simple. Speak to him, I'm sure he knows something.'

'We sent an officer to the Caledonia Dreaming office earlier, but he wasn't available.'

'Wasn't available? Jesus, this isn't jury service, it's a murder investigation.'

'It's a matter of limited resources.'

'This is my wife we're talking about.'

'I understand your concern.'

'Do you really?'

'Mr Douglas . . .'

'I don't think you understand a fucking thing. How many murder investigations have you been a part of?'

'That's hardly relevant.'

'I think it's absolutely relevant.'

'I'm trained in all manner of police investigations.'

Mark scratched the top of his head. 'Can I speak to your superior about this, that Inspector Green?'

'There's no need for this hostility, Mr Douglas. If you'll just let us get on with the investigation, we'll keep you updated as soon as we have any more information.'

Mark puffed out a handful of deep breaths. 'OK, there's something else. When can I have Lauren's body for the funeral?'

'I'll look into it for you. Now they've completed the full post-mortem, I see no reason why the body can't be released to you soon.'

'The body.' Mark didn't mean to say it out loud.

'I'm sorry.'

Mark lifted the phone away from his ear and stared at it. He ended the call and walked through the flat to find Nathan. The boy was lying on his bed, reading a *Clone Wars* comic. One minute devastated, the next seemingly fine. How long would this shit go on, the rest of their lives?

'We're going out.'

'Where are we going?'

'Just out.'

'Can I bring my DS?'

'Sure.'

'I'm hungry, Daddy.'

'We'll get a Maccy D on the way.'

Lauren wouldn't be happy about that. Tough. That's what you got when you died and left people behind, you gave up your chance to have a say in their lives.

Nathan jumped off his bed and went for his DS.

Mark dug his car key out his pocket and headed for the door.

*

Squally rain was spattering against the windscreen as he pulled

157

in down the road from Caledonia Dreaming. The kind of rain that just got smudged across the glass, rather than cleared away by the wipers. Mark switched the engine off. The car was shuddering in the wind. When was it ever going to stop?

He ducked out and found a parking meter. Dug for change. Didn't know how long he was going to be here. Just stuffed it all in the machine, pressed green. Scurried back to the car and stuck his ticket on the windscreen.

Nathan was licking salt off his fingers from the fries.

'Come on,' Mark said.

Nathan picked up his Fruit Shoot and his DS and squirmed out of the car into the rain. 'Where are we going?'

Mark pointed. 'There.'

'Mummy's work? Why?'

'Never mind. Let's go.'

They blustered into reception. Same snooty bitch at the desk. Mark pushed Nathan towards the cream sofa. The boy got his DS out and flipped it open, stuck his feet on a coffee table.

'Hello again,' Mark said to the receptionist.

She looked terrified.

'I take it you've heard about my wife.'

'I'm sorry.'

'What are you sorry for?' He was pushing it, but fuck it. Fuck it all. Fuck this privileged bitch and everyone like her.

The girl was like a baby deer looking for its mummy.

'I want to speak to Gavin Taylor,' Mark said, voice low.

The girl frowned. 'Mr Taylor is not available right now.'

'I don't give a shit if he's available or not, just tell me if he's in the office.'

The girl's eyes darted, a quick glance at the doorway opposite. That was all Mark needed.

'Nathan, stay here with this nice lady. I'll be back in a minute.'

Nathan looked up then put his head back down to the console.

Mark strode towards the office. The girl didn't even shout after him.

Down the corridor, remembering the last time he was here, when Lauren had only been missing for half a day. Everything had collapsed in on itself since then.

But something had hardened inside him, something vital. He could do this now. He would find out.

He pushed the door open without knocking and there was Taylor already lifting himself out of his seat.

'Mark, I'm so sorry to hear about Lauren.'

'Why haven't you talked to the police?'

'What?'

'I just called one of the investigating detectives, she said you hadn't spoken to them yet.'

'Mark, sit down.'

'I'd rather stand if it's all the same.'

They were only a couple of feet away from each other. Mark felt energy flowing through him, like he was a lightning rod.

Taylor had a wary look in his eyes and his body was tense, ready for a fight if it came to it.

'It's just a misunderstanding,' he said. 'They called when I was out at a meeting. I called them back but the officer wasn't around. I'll give them a statement as soon as I can.'

'What do you know?'

'I told you everything when you were here the other day.

Lauren came in for the morning then headed off because she had a half day.'

'Were you fucking her?'

'What?'

'You heard me. Were you fucking her?'

'Mark, I think you need to . . .'

'I'll ask you one last time. Did you fuck Lauren?'

Mark's jaw was clenched, his arms rigid.

'No, Mark, I never went near her.'

'I can find out.'

'What do you mean?'

'I've got all her passwords, I can check her emails, Facebook and Twitter messages going back years. If there's anything in there between you and her, I'll find it.'

'You won't find anything.'

Mark stared into Taylor's eyes. He thought he could see something there.

'I can tell you're lying.'

'I'm not lying.'

'You think the police won't find out what happened?'

'Mark, you have to calm down. I could have you arrested for coming in here and threatening me like this.'

'Go on, get the police. Then we'll see who's telling the truth.'

Taylor put his hands out. Calm down and all that. Mark wanted to grab him and stab him through the neck with a pencil.

'Just take it easy.' Taylor was using a quiet voice, it was meant to be reassuring.

Mark grabbed Taylor by the arms and pushed, trying to knock him off balance. But Taylor was a rock, immovable.

Mark swung a fist towards his head but he was too slow. Taylor swerved to avoid it then let Mark follow through, his looping arm shifting his centre of gravity and making him unsteady. Taylor shoved and Mark staggered forwards until he slammed into the wall. Taylor turned him round and pushed a forearm across his throat so he couldn't breathe. He kicked Mark's legs apart and tucked his knee just below his exposed groin, ready to do damage. Mark was beaten and it had taken less than five seconds.

Mark gasped for air, scrabbling at the arm pressed against his throat, but Taylor held firm.

'I'm sorry about Lauren.' Taylor's voice was still low and soft, like he was reading a lullaby at bedtime. 'But I have nothing else to say to you.'

Mark tried to glean something from Taylor, some sign of guilt, some hint of a secret, but the truth was he couldn't see anything.

Taylor released the pressure on his windpipe and Mark slumped to the floor. Taylor stood over him, the victor over the defeated foe.

'I think you'd better leave. Now.'

29

They waited. He had another hour on his ticket, they'd eaten, and Nathan had his DS, so why not? Only problems could be if the boy needed a piss or the DS's battery ran out. After ten minutes Mark decided they were too close to the office, too obvious, so he drove round the square and came back. Found a space further away, but still with a sightline to the front door.

Mark stared at the Caledonia Dreaming office. He zoned out, his mind going over unspeakable things in his head. He pictured Taylor screwing Lauren from behind, her laughing, the two of them sniggering at their deceit afterwards, sharing a joint like Mark and Lauren used to back in the days before Nathan, the days before the routine of family life, the days before one of them would wash up cold and blue and clammy on the beach.

It was easier to be angry than sad. Wallowing in grief was what teenagers did. If he could blame Lauren for everything, make it her fault that she was dead, then he would be lifted up from the bottom of the pit by his own righteous fury.

No, he mustn't think like that. It was already poisoning his memory of her, which would in turn destroy Nathan's relationship with her. He had to keep it together, for the boy's sake. Ruth was right about that.

'Daddy?'

His mind was hauled back into the car. The cantina song from *Star Wars* was playing. Didn't someone get his arm cut off in that scene? And Harrison Ford shot a guy as well. Some bounty hunter.

'What is it?'

'Do you know what I can do as a clone?'

'What?'

'Press X and aim at a battle droid's head, and it plants a bomb in there.'

'Very good.'

Nathan was giggling. 'They run around mad for a bit then lie on the ground and their heads explode.'

'Really?'

Clones and battle droids, that was the newer films. Yet the cantina music was playing. That was all mixed up, surely? Mark wondered if he should say something about the violence. But Nathan got it, didn't he?

'It's OK, Daddy, they're not real.'

As if the boy could read his mind. That happened so much these days, both ways. Nathan would start a question with 'I know the answer's no, Daddy, but can I . . .' When they played rock-paper-scissors, Mark knew what Nathan was going to do with his hand every single time. How could two people be so close? How could they have so much knowledge of each other? Infinitely more than he could ever have imagined possible.

The birth of Nathan had made him feel physically sick at the thought of how much he'd taken his own dad for granted, even worse because his dad wasn't around any more. Mark's typical teenage strops and moody shit must've been so insulting to his dad, he realised, an affront to everything the man had done for him. Mark had never had the chance to acknowledge that before he died.

At least Lauren would be spared the indignity of having her son insult her that way. But that was a horrible thing to think, because that was all part of it, all part of the bullshit of parenthood.

At five o'clock Taylor came out the office and bustled down the steps. The rain was off and the wind had died a little but it was still bothering the tops of trees into a skirmish of leaves. Taylor was surprisingly fast for a big man as he slipped into his Lexus.

Mark started the engine and followed from as far back as he could. He didn't know why but he had to do something. Anything was better than going home and just sitting there.

Taylor took the same route up Lothian Road and through Tollcross then round the Meadows, Mark hanging back but keeping him in sight. The Lexus took an unexpected right in Marchmont, then another right along a cobbled street into Bruntsfield.

Mark knew the area well, round the corner was where he and Lauren had owned their first flat together, a one-bedroom, third-floor box with rattling windows and no central heating. When Lauren got pregnant with Nathan, they had to look further afield to find a place they could afford with a second bedroom, and had ended up in Porty along with hundreds of other displaced young parents.

Mark followed the Lexus round Bruntsfield Links, the criss-crossing paths across the park full of girls in leggings and loose tops, boys in skinny jeans, students traipsing and skipping home from university classes.

Taylor pulled in to the kerb and stopped. Mark's heart thudded. Why was Taylor stopping here? This wasn't his home. Mark drove on past the car, angling his face away in case he got noticed, then turned round the next corner. He kept driving, left and left again round the block, until he emerged a hundred yards behind the parked Lexus.

He pulled in, switched the engine off and waited. Tried to breathe steadily.

'Daddy, you know how Anakin turns into Darth Vader?'

'Yeah.' Mark reached for the *Star Wars* binoculars still lying on the passenger seat.

Nathan kept his head down, concentrating on the game. 'Well, it's a bit strange.'

'What's strange?' Mark focused the binoculars. Taylor was crossing the road towards the park, his back to Mark. Where the hell was he going, a walk in the park on his way home? Didn't make sense.

'He starts off as a goodie,' Nathan said, 'but then he turns into a baddie.'

'That's right.' Mark watched as Taylor approached a park bench where a man was sitting. The man was about the same age as Taylor, with a hard, lived-in face and an expensive leather jacket. He was playing with a dog lead, and a Jack Russell was sniffing nearby trees. The dog was incongruous – the man was bigger than Taylor and looked tough, pockmarked cheeks and thick fists. The kind of man you would expect to have a Staffy or a Rotty, one of those hardman mutts.

'But then even as a baddie, he saves Luke and kills the Emperor at the end.'

'Yeah.'

Taylor sat down next to the man, who didn't turn round, just kept staring straight ahead. The binoculars drifted a little out of focus, and Mark rolled them back into sharpness.

'So which is he, a goodie or a baddie?'

Taylor began talking, not looking round. But this was clearly a meeting, not an accident, and the fact they weren't looking at each other meant it was supposed to be a secret.

This was something.

Mark felt his neck flush with blood. This was really something.

'He's kind of both, Big Guy. It's a bit complicated. Sometimes people can be goodies and baddies.'

Taylor was still talking, getting more animated. He turned to look at the hardman a couple of times, got a curt word from him for his trouble. Dribs and drabs of students were drifting by, mucking about like they owned the future.

'That's just confusing,' Nathan said.

Taylor didn't stop. He was waving his hands around now, running fingers across his stubbled scalp, agitated.

'Yeah, life can be confusing sometimes,' Mark said.

Eventually the hardman had heard enough, and threw out a gloved hand to Taylor's neck. Taylor froze. The hardman turned and spoke calmly through clenched teeth. Mark thought of that scene with Darth Vader in *Star Wars*, where he chokes one of the other guys round the table. 'I find your lack of faith disturbing,' or whatever. Although of course Vader never needed to touch the guy. Christ, Mark was watching too much *Star Wars*.

The hardman let go of Taylor, who looked like he was about

to piss himself. Did this have anything to do with Lauren? How could he find out?

Taylor got up and said something to the other guy, putting a brave face on his submission, then he turned and walked back to his car. Mark lowered the binoculars. A student couple walked past the Peugeot and clocked him with the toy binoculars in his hands, giving him funny looks and whispering. He wanted to tell them they had no idea what life had in store for them, it would grind them into dust.

Up ahead, the Lexus pulled out, trundling over the cobbles.

The hardman clicked his fingers once and the Jack Russell trotted over and got its lead on. The man stood up and walked west towards the top of Bruntsfield and Morningside. He had a calm, methodical gait. Now the man was standing, Mark could see he was wearing a tailored shirt, chinos and leather shoes. He was well over six feet and several stone heavier than Mark. A lot of muscle.

Mark turned to Nathan.

'Come on.'

'Where are we going?' Nathan was already shutting his DS and undoing his seatbelt.

Mark looked. The man was a hundred yards away now, heading for Bruntsfield Place. 'A sweetie shop.'

'Why?'

A sweetie shop was shorthand between them for any corner shop, really. Anywhere that had lollipops or cola bottles or something sour. Nathan was going through a phase of sour sweets, he liked to feel the sharpness of them on his tongue.

'To get you a sweetie for being so good and waiting patiently in the car.'

Nathan bounded out and they walked through the park, following the man and his dog. Nathan kept leaping about, running on ahead. Mark tried to calm him, worried he would draw attention.

They got to the road. They were catching up on the man because he was walking slowly. Speed up, you dick. They approached a corner shop.

'Is this the sweetie shop?'

'No.'

'But this one has sweeties.'

There was a big display in the window, of course.

The man was up at the turning for Morningside.

'There's a better one further ahead.'

'Aw.'

The man turned up Colinton Road then eventually down Napier Road. Wide street, big trees, even bigger houses. Made Taylor's neighbourhood look like Craigmillar. A real millionaires' row. Mark was sure he'd heard that J. K. Rowling lived round here somewhere. A lot was made of Morningside's reputation, but that was more about old-school snootiness. The real Edinburgh money lived here in Merchiston.

The man stopped at the driveway of one of the properties, a large closed gate in front of him. He pressed a button and spoke to someone through an intercom system, then the gate slid open with a whir. He sauntered through, the Jack Russell trotting along obediently. The gate closed behind them.

'Daddy, there's no sweetie shops in this street.'

Mark looked at the house. 'No, you're right, I made a mistake.'

Nathan tugged on his hand. 'Silly Daddy.'

Mark looked at him. 'Just a minute.'

He jogged up the road to the driveway entrance. Looked up at the huge spikes along the top of the gate's railings. Noticed a brass plate on a stone pillar to the side. Number 40.

He turned and walked back to Nathan. He had a street name and a house number. That was something to start with.

'Can I have a sour snake if they have any?' Nathan said.

Mark took the boy's hand. 'You can have two.'

30

Back at the car, a quick search on his phone came up with some info. Number 40 Napier Road had been bought by its current owners three months ago. They paid one and a half million for it. Strange thing was, it wasn't an individual but a company, Fisher Holdings. Some sort of property developer, although that part was vague. Clearly someone was doing well, despite the economic collapse and the recent drop in house prices. He rooted around some more and found out that Fisher Holdings was owned by Innes Fisher. Pulled up a picture and zoomed in. It was him, the hardman with the leather gloves and the yappy dog.

But what did he have to do with Taylor, how did they know each other? Why go and meet him in the park, not in an office or at his home? That was the good part, the part that made Mark think there was something in this.

Did it have anything to do with Lauren, though? He wondered if what he was doing was part of the grieving process. Mental displacement. He'd read about it after Lauren's dad died. Lauren had become briefly obsessed with self-improvement, going to the gym, buying self-help books. Of course, all that was before she dug up the buried nightmare of what her father had done.

But this wasn't displacement, there really was something to find out.

Lauren had been murdered.

Strangled.

He thought of Fisher's gloved hand on Taylor's throat. He could see the fine stitching, could imagine the creak of the fawn leather as he squeezed, the rasp of Taylor's breath as he struggled to get oxygen into his blood.

Strangled, Jesus.

New guilt came swarming in around him, suffocating him. The first thing he'd thought of when he saw Fisher grabbing Taylor wasn't his dead wife but Darth Vader. Darth fucking Vader. What did that say about his priorities, about his mind-set?

His eyes filled with tears. Nathan in the back of the car hadn't noticed. Mark swivelled the heels of his hands in his eye sockets and sniffed.

'Are you OK, Daddy?'

He took an uneven breath. 'Just thinking about Mummy, that's all.'

'I miss her too.'

'I know you do, Big Guy.'

A pause, but Mark knew Nathan wasn't finished. He just knew.

'But we still have each other, don't we?' the boy said.

Fuck. He wanted to hold the boy, but they were both strapped into their seats. He turned, not bothering to hide the tears.

'Yes, we still have each other.'

Nathan had a resigned smile on his face. He leaned forward and patted Mark's shoulder. 'It's OK, Daddy.'

Mark put a hand on the boy's fingers and squeezed.

*

They shared a fish supper on their knees in front of *Horrible Histories*. Salt and vinegar on it, Lauren would've frowned at that. Salt on chips at his age. A McDonald's and a chippy on the same day, Nathan must be wishing his mum died more often.

What a terrible thing to think. Why couldn't he stop this shit from infecting his brain? Grief wasn't the towering misery it was always portrayed as, he knew that from the death of his own dad when he was a teenager. He knew it even more now. Only him, Nathan and Ruth left to grieve, the family almost wiped off the planet.

Mark's dad dying seemed like a lifetime ago. Mark was just a kid really, he hadn't known how to handle it, and hadn't cared much either. He'd drifted along for a while until he moved to Edinburgh and met Lauren. Started a new life. A new life that was over now as well. Time to move on to life number three, just father and son. But not until he found out who was responsible for all this.

On the television, two Celts were having a boast battle about how many enemies they'd killed. More violence. Mark remembered the first time Nathan had made a gun shape with his hand, pointed it at Lauren and said 'Bang'. Just past two years old. Something picked up from older boys at nursery. Always the boys.

Mark and Lauren had been shocked, but once that floodgate

was opened, that was it – toy guns, swords, an awareness of boxing and wrestling, violence in cartoons and, of course, lightsabers and blasters. But so what? It turned out you didn't need all that shit to kill someone, all you needed was a pair of strong hands and some serious willpower.

The buzzer went. Mark couldn't even think who it might be. He went to answer it.

'Mr Douglas?'

He knew the voice. Ferguson. 'Have you found out something about Lauren's murderer?'

'Can we come up, please?'

He buzzed her in and opened the door.

She was with a different sidekick this time, the uniformed kid from the reception desk at the station. He was about twenty with bumfluff on his face and a line of spots along a crease in his forehead that reminded Mark of Vyvyan from *The Young Ones*. He wondered if the kid was born when that was on television. Worked it out and realised the show was on ten years before this kid was even alive. Fucking Jesus.

He let them in and ushered them to the other end of the hall from the living room.

'I'm glad you're here, I have something to tell you. I saw Taylor today, he's definitely into something dodgy.'

Ferguson pushed a strand of hair behind her ear. 'You went to see Gavin Taylor again?'

'Well you didn't seem to be trying too hard to talk to him.'

'I strongly advise you to leave the investigating to us, Mr Douglas.'

'I would if you were actually doing any investigating.'

'We are progressing as fast as resources allow.'

'In other words, doing nothing.'

'Mr Douglas, that's not helpful.'

'I followed him, and I saw him meet someone in Bruntsfield Links.'

'You followed him?'

'A guy called Innes Fisher, do you know him? He lives in Napier Road, number 40. The place is a mansion. He's obviously doing well for himself. Maybe he's into something criminal. Can you run his name through the police computer or something?'

'Mr Douglas, we're not here about your wife's death.'

That pulled Mark up. 'What?'

'We've had a formal complaint about you.'

'From who?'

'Mrs Kelly Robertson.'

Mark shook his head. 'Never heard of her.'

'She claims you assaulted her yesterday afternoon in the infant playground of Towerbank Primary School.'

Lee's mum. Shit. 'That was nothing.'

'She says you punched her in the face in full view of pupils, parents and staff.'

'It was a misunderstanding.'

'We've got plenty of witnesses to confirm her statement, Mr Douglas.'

'I'm sure you do.'

'This is extremely serious.'

'As serious as finding my wife's killer?'

'In light of Mrs Robertson's statement, you're going to have to come back down to the station and answer some more questions.'

Mark shook his head. 'You're fucking joking me.'

'I'm afraid not,' Ferguson said.

Mark listened through to the living room. *Horrible Histories* was still on. He could hear the Grim Reaper singing 'Stupid Deaths'. One of the boy's favourites.

'What about Nathan?'

Ferguson shrugged. 'Same as before. Either get a babysitter or bring him and a social worker will sit with him.'

'What if I refuse to come?'

'Then we'll formally arrest you right now and take you anyway.'

Mark shook his head. He looked at the spotty kid copper. He had no clue about life yet, none whatsoever. Neither did Ferguson. How quickly it could shit on you from a great height and all you could do was smile and say thanks.

'That doesn't really give me much choice, does it?'

Same interview room as before, same scratchy carpet and squeaky chairs. No scrapping gulls outside the window this time, though.

Ferguson and Green sat opposite, Ferguson fiddling with the digital recorder, Green clicking a cheap pen. Mark had already been advised he was under caution but not under arrest. Ferguson read him his rights, straight off a TV cop show. He waved away the offer of a duty solicitor when it was explained that it might take several hours to find one. Nathan was in a room downstairs with a social worker. Mark had phoned Ruth but just got her voicemail.

'Can we get this over with,' he said. 'I just want to get home with my son.'

'This is a very serious situation,' Ferguson said.

Mark pinched the bridge of his nose. 'You don't say.'

Ferguson stopped fiddling with the recorder and laid it on the desk.

'So tell us what happened at Towerbank,' she said.

'We're really doing this?' Mark said.

Ferguson nodded.

'Look, I admit I slapped her,' he said.

Green pointed at the machine. 'Could you speak up for the recording.'

Mark stared at him. 'I admit I might have slapped Lee's mum.'

'She said it was more than a slap,' Ferguson said. 'She had to go to hospital to check whether or not her nose was broken.'

'Was it?'

'That's not the point,' Ferguson said. 'So you are admitting you assaulted Mrs Robertson?'

Mark thought for a moment. 'Things got out of hand, that's all.'

'Out of hand in what way?'

'Her son was hitting Nathan. There's your assault. I just went over to stop him.'

'Mrs Robertson said Nathan was the one who instigated the fight with her son.'

'Mrs Robertson is a fucking liar. If you knew Nathan at all, you'd know that's not like him.'

'So what happened in the playground?'

'I broke the boys up,' Mark said. 'She came over and started mouthing off.'

'So you hit her.'

Mark dragged his hands down his face. 'I know I shouldn't have, OK? I'm not some knuckle-dragging moron. I'd just found out about Lauren, for Christ's sake. I wasn't thinking straight. Surely that has to be taken into account.'

Ferguson glanced at Green. 'There are obvious mitigating circumstances,' she said. 'But this remains a very serious matter. We're still collecting witness statements, but you'll likely be charged with assault. If found guilty, you could even face a custodial sentence. Social services will have to be involved.'

Mark scratched at his neck then put his hands out.

'Wait a minute, let's not go mad here. I'm all Nathan's got. I made a mistake, I admit that. I'll apologise to her, whatever it takes. I'll explain to her about Lauren.'

Green sat forward. 'Yes, Lauren. We need to talk about that.' He slumped back, as if the effort of speaking was too much.

Mark looked at him.

'What about it? Do you have some more information? Did you speak to Taylor?'

Green shook his head. 'We need you to talk us through your exact movements on the day your wife went missing.'

'What?'

Ferguson spoke. 'We're trying to help you.'

Mark shook his head. 'It doesn't sound like it.'

Green's turn. 'In light of Mrs Robertson's claims, our focus has shifted.'

'Because I slapped a shitty school-mum bitch, now you think I strangled my wife?'

Ferguson tilted her head. 'Look at it from our point of view. We're now aware of you committing two serious assaults. You've attended anger management classes under court order. Your father-in-law went missing years ago and turned up dead. The same man who abused your wife when she was a child. And now your wife has been murdered.'

'No, I'm not having this. I explained about both times I hit someone. I've only ever done that twice. And I already explained that we didn't know about William abusing Lauren when he went missing. Anyway, what fucking reason would I have for killing Lauren?'

'That's what we're trying to establish,' Green said.

'Fuck you,' Mark said, voice shaking. 'No reason, OK? No fucking reason. I loved my wife and I want her back.'

Mark was standing up, fists pressed down on the table. Green pushed his chair back in readiness.

'Sit down,' he said.

Mark looked from him to Ferguson then down at his knuckles, skin stretched tight. He eased himself back into his chair.

'So,' Green said. 'Talk us through the day your wife went missing.'

Mark sighed. 'She left for work around half eight. I took Nathan to school. Then I went home. Didn't do much in the morning except go to the shop for milk, watch TV and go on-line for a bit.'

'When did you start work?'

'I was on the backshift, started at two. I didn't go into the office because I knew my first job was to photograph the whales, no point slogging into town just to head back out.'

Ferguson and Green exchanged a look. Ferguson picked up a piece of paper and studied it briefly, although she clearly already knew what was on it.

'You didn't start until two?'

'That's right.'

'And you were on Portobello beach from then until when?'

'Until I got the call from Towerbank about Nathan at three thirty. We've been through all this a million times.'

'Lauren was last seen at the Caledonia Dreaming office at 12.20 p.m.'

'So?'

'So what were you doing between 12.20 p.m. and 2?'

Mark's whole body was rigid. 'I was at home, probably eating a sandwich and watching *Loose Women* or some other shit, I don't know.'

Green folded his arms. 'Did anyone see you between those two times?'

'Not unless they were spying on me through the window.'

'How were things between you and Lauren prior to her disappearance?'

Mark's hands on the table began to tremble. 'I've told you all this already. Me and Lauren were fine. I had nothing to do with her going missing and to be honest I feel sick at the thought of what you're implying.'

'Did you ever argue?' Green said.

'No more than any other couple.'

'Is that a little or a lot? What are we talking about here?'

Mark waved a hand, exasperated. 'Hardly ever.'

'Did you ever hit her?' Green's face was deadpan.

Mark breathed out. 'No. How dare you.'

'Well you've hit two other women. That we know of.'

'Fuck you.'

Ferguson raised a placating hand. 'Please, Mr Douglas.'

'No.' Mark stood up again. His legs felt liquid, like he might collapse. 'I've had enough of this. I came here willingly, but this is bullshit. I had no reason to do any harm to Lauren, and I resent you suggesting it. I want to leave, take my son home and put him to bed. So either charge me with something right now or I'm leaving.'

Ferguson looked at Green, who nodded.

'OK, you can go,' Ferguson said. 'But expect to hear from us soon.'

32

Bedtime was a nightmare.

'I'm not tired.'

'Doesn't matter.'

This went on for ages. Mark tried to put the interview to the back of his mind. He was itching to get back on his phone, spend a few hours looking into Innes Fisher and Caledonia Dreaming. See if he could find a connection. He tried not to think about Lee's mum, the trouble she could cause. Social services. Assault. All of it.

'Bed.'

'Don't want to.'

'Stop being a little brat and get your jammies on.'

'No.'

Mark lost it and shouted. As loud as he could, right in Nathan's face. The boy's body slumped and his face crumpled, tears ran down his cheeks. It was instantaneous.

Mark tried to hold him. 'I'm sorry, Big Guy.'

But Nathan pushed him away. With sudden focus in his eyes, the boy leaned back, pursed his lips and spat in Mark's face.

Mark slapped him without thinking.

Not hard. But hard enough.

Nathan's eyes widened for a moment, then he swung a fist

at Mark who caught his arm easily. Another fist came and Mark grabbed the boy's other wrist. He was holding on tight, too tight, could feel the sinews running along the bones of Nathan's arms, could feel the muscles tensing under his grip.

Nathan raised a foot and slammed his heel into Mark's shin, the kind of kick that was a leg-breaking tackle in football. Luckily the boy was just in his socks. Mark grabbed Nathan round his waist and pulled him tight to his own body, felt the boy's arms and legs thrashing, Nathan's little fists pounding on his back and head as he screamed and cried and gulped for air.

'It's all your fault.'

'Calm down.' Mark tried to keep his voice quiet. He couldn't even hear himself over Nathan's tantrum.

'You killed Mummy.'

'Take it easy.'

Mark had a flash to when Nathan was a baby, the sleepless nights, the incomprehensible screaming, the constant shushing and rocking and comforting. He remembered having the occasional insane, evil thought. About what he could do to make this baby quiet, to make him stop. Thoughts he'd never mentioned to Lauren because he knew they would shock her, even after her depression. Thoughts that sickened him.

He squeezed hold of Nathan now, felt the tremors coursing through the boy, the uneven twitches of his chest as he tried to breathe between sobs. Mark's own chest was heaving as well, tears wetting his cheeks, running into Nathan's hair, the boy's head pulled tight to his chest under Mark's big hand. Mark had to do this alone now, he was the guiding light for this kid in the world, him alone, without Lauren. And he was slapping him and shouting at him.

Gradually Nathan calmed down as Mark slumped to the floor and rocked the pair of them for an age, his mind seeing the curve of Lauren's hip resting on the sand, Fisher's gloved hand on Taylor's throat.

Mark stroked the boy's head, that unruly tussle of hair.

'I'm sorry. I'm so sorry.'

He released Nathan from the embrace. Tears and snot had made a mess of the boy's face, his eyes puffy from crying, his skin flushed. Mark tried to see if there was a mark. Ran his fingers softly across the boy's cheek.

'I'm sorry I slapped you.'

Nathan wiped at his eyes and nose with his sleeve.

'It's OK, Daddy. I'm sorry I said that about Mummy.'

It was like something from one of Nathan's Be Responsible classes at school, anti-bullying, good behaviour initiatives that were rife in the classroom, trying to shape model citizens, everyone being nice and apologising all the time.

'We have to stick together, Big Guy.'

'Now that we don't have Mummy, you mean.'

'Exactly.'

Mark pulled a tissue out his pocket and wiped Nathan's eyes for him, then his own, then did both their noses, making a joke of it.

'Now it really is time to get your jammies on.'

Nathan put on puppy eyes. 'Can I sleep in your bed again, Daddy?'

'Of course.' Mark wondered how long that would go on for, and realised he didn't give a shit. It could go on forever for all he cared.

The boy picked out *The Zax* for his bedtime story, another

Dr Seuss one. A simple moral about the perils of being stubborn. Like the whole Middle East conflict summed up in zany primary colours.

Mark uncoupled his brain from the story as he read. He had to think about Caledonia Dreaming. About whether Lauren was involved in something, or if she was just randomly killed by a stranger. That seemed unacceptable, as if the killer had to have had a reason. Conditioning from too many crime dramas on television, all neatly wrapped up in an hour or two, motives and opportunity, forensics and resolution. But real life didn't work like that. Sometimes there was no answer, no resolution.

'Daddy?'

Mark realised he'd finished the story and was just sitting there with the book open at the last page, the two Zax standing there nose to nose, arguing away, as the whole world went on around them, not giving a flying shit.

'Sorry, in a daydream there.'

They kissed goodnight then Mark put Vaseline on the boy's chapped lips, trying not to think about Lauren's lips as he smeared it on.

He noticed that Nathan had placed the piece of sea glass on the bedside table, sitting on top of Lauren's pile of books. The boy was staring at it as Mark left the room, the bedside light still on.

Mark went to the kitchen, opened a beer and rubbed at his eyes. He walked through the flat then slumped on a sofa in the living room and got on the internet on his phone. No laptop. Started searching for anything on Fisher, Taylor and Caledonia Dreaming. Just a world of bland, corporate jargon with nothing of interest. He rooted around social media and a few chatrooms and blogs, seeing if anyone had mentioned them in a derogatory light. But there seemed to be no bad stuff, no disgruntled employees, no unhappy customers. Fisher had bought his mansion recently for piles of cash, the kind of high-end property Caledonia Dreaming dealt with. Was that the only link? Taylor had sold Fisher his house? But why meet up in the park, why be secretive about it, an hour after Mark had confronted Taylor? Coincidence? And why the aggression between them?

After the fourth beer, his eyes grew sore from staring at the tiny screen. He was no nearer an answer. He threw his phone down.

He tried to think good things about Lauren, tried to remember the best times. Their first trip to T in the Park together, back when it was at Strathclyde Country Park and the organisation was a shambles. They'd parked and pitched a tent next to the pond, shared their first ever Ecstasy and gone to see the Prodigy. Then there was their first holiday together, a cheap deal to Prague before it was full of stag and hen nights. Walking along the famous bridge that had just featured in the first *Mission Impossible* film, eating stew and dumplings and drinking strong lager, wandering around the cobbled streets in a daze of love. He was swamped by firsts – their first date, the first time they had sex, the first time they said 'I love you', the first time he met her parents, the first time they shared a flat, the first place they bought, the first dance at their wedding. Their first child.

Their only child.

It just hurt. It was just scratching at a massive, gaping wound in his and Nathan's lives. It was just pain, pure pain. Nothing more.

He staggered through to the bedroom and lay down on the covers next to Nathan. He could smell him, that unique, animal scent he had. Six years old already, bony limbs and spindly hands. His jammies were too small, Mark would need to get new ones. Was it that easy, just getting on with life after Lauren? Buy jammies, get haircut, cook tea, keep breathing and crying and pissing and shitting and feeling the giant hole in their lives all the while.

Nathan now had the sea glass gripped in his fist as he slept. Mark put his hand in his own pocket and rubbed at the baby teeth in there. He made a wish. A wish that could never come true.

He closed his eyes and tried to think of a future.

33

He was standing waist deep in the sea at Portobello embracing Lauren, both of them naked. He kissed her, caressed her buttocks, then entered her. Their skin and flesh began to fall away from their bodies but it wasn't horrific, it was a relief not to be burdened by all that weight. Their skeletons dissolved until they were just ghosts standing there, still interlocked. Then their spirits entered the water and were dispersed around the oceans of the world.

Voices.

Not a dream any more, real voices. He snapped awake and sat up. Nathan's heavy breathing in the room. Whispers were coming from somewhere else in the flat. He got up and crept to the bedroom door. Listened. Couldn't hear anything.

He remembered last time, the break-in, how he'd thought it was Lauren.

Not this time.

He tried to think.

His phone. He'd left it on the sofa in the living room last night. Still there.

He went to the wardrobe and slowly pulled the drawer open. Rummaged inside and lifted out the gun box. Got the key from his pocket, unlocked it and took the shammy cloth out. Unwrapped the Browning and clicked the magazine out. He stopped a moment to listen. Still no voices, just the sound of Nathan breathing. He began sliding the bullets into the magazine, squeezing them in with his thumb. When they were all in he eased the magazine back in.

He crept towards the door. Pressed his ear against it. Nothing. His own shallow breaths, that was all.

He reached out and touched the door handle. Every nerve in his body was singing. He turned the handle and pulled the door open just enough. Darkness in the hallway, the front door closed, a thin spread of light from the stairwell seeping underneath.

He looked back at Nathan, still sound asleep.

He opened the bedroom door just enough to squeeze through, then inched into the hallway.

Caught a smell of something, alcohol, then felt a crushing pain against the left side of his skull. He slumped to the floor, his legs gone beneath him. He tried to grab at the bedroom door handle on the way down. Managed to tug the door almost closed, hiding Nathan, but the gun slipped from his hand as he fell.

He looked up. There was a zigzag of torch beams, spotlights shooting around, strafing the walls and ceiling. A short man in a grey hoodie was standing over him. A kitchen knife in one hand and a heavy torch in the other. Mark tried to focus but his eyes were wet, the pain bringing tears. His gun was under his foot.

He felt himself being dragged along the ground by a second pair of hands. As he moved away, he flicked at the gun with his foot, knocking it a couple of feet into the corner of the hallway. He was dragged into the living room, the guy in the grey hoodie following behind. In the darkness, the guy hadn't noticed the gun over by the skirting board.

Mark was dragged to the desk chair. The two men lifted him into it. Mark could see now that the second guy was bigger and wore a dark blue hoodie. Was he the same guy from the first break-in? He pulled an electrical cable from his pocket and tied Mark's hands behind his back with it.

'What the fuck do you think you're doing?' Mark said.

The guy in the blue hoodie slapped him hard on the side of the face. The other side from the torch blow. The pain seemed to meet in the middle of his skull, and he shook his head trying to dislodge it.

He squeezed his eyes shut and pictured Nathan sprawled over the covers in the next room.

He had to keep the men in here. Had to.

When he opened his eyes, the desk lamp was on. He could see them better. Both in dark jeans, hoodies pulled tight and wearing dust masks on their faces, so he could only see their eyes. He didn't know if that was good or bad. If he couldn't identify them, maybe they would let him live.

'What's this about?' he said.

Blue stepped forward and threw a punch into Mark's stomach, winding him. He struggled to open his throat, take a breath in, but it wouldn't come. Five seconds, more, then he gasped and rocked with the throbbing pain in his gut.

Grey came up to him. He was skinny and shorter. He stank of whisky and hash. He punched Mark in the cheek, a clumsy strike, but a sovereign ring on his middle finger broke the skin at Mark's cheekbone and he felt blood seeping down his face, dripping on to his neck.

Grey stepped back and leaned against the desk, arms crossed.

'Let's make this simple,' he said, voice slightly muffled by the mask. 'What's the password?'

'What?'

A backhand swing at his other cheek made his neck crack. The pain was swarming all over him now.

'If you just tell us, we can all get on with our lives.'

Mark looked from Grey to Blue. 'I honestly don't know what you're talking about. Just take whatever you want and leave. I won't tell the police.'

The men looked at each other. Blue leaned forward and landed several more punches to Mark's stomach and side. Mark squirmed and writhed in his seat, feeling the screaming of his internal organs.

Grey spoke. 'We just want the password.'

This was about Lauren. It wasn't random. He wasn't going mad. Despite the pain across his body, he felt triumphant. Vindicated.

'I don't know what you mean.'

Grey approached Mark with the knife, like a playground bully with a stick.

'Don't think we won't torture you, because we will. We've got instructions.'

Mark thought about that. 'Who sent you? Taylor? Fisher?'

Grey narrowed his eyes then looked at Blue. Did that mean something? Was it recognition?

Grey pointed the knife at Mark, brought the tip of it closer to his neck. Mark strained his head away from the blade, but he couldn't move any further, constricted by his hands tied to the chair. He felt the cold metal of the knife against his throat, then felt the blade break the skin, just a cut, a release of tension as blood dribbled down his neck and on to his T-shirt.

Grey grabbed Mark's scalp and gripped tight, then began trying to push his head down, forcing his neck against the blade, which sank another tiny amount into the flesh. Mark could feel his pulse in his throat, the adrenalin coursing through his arteries as blood leaked out of him, the knife tip at his neck, just inches away from killing him.

The main light in the room came on.

'Get away from my daddy.'

Grey let go of Mark's hair and turned.

Nathan was standing in the doorway pointing the Browning at Grey. Two hands, shaking. The gun was swaying around, outsized in his tiny grip. Grey lowered the knife and put his other hand out.

'Well, if it isn't the runt of the family.'

'Leave him alone,' Mark said.

Grey shook his head. Blue was just watching, turning his head between his partner and the boy, soaking it in.

Grey took a step towards Nathan.

'Leave him alone.' Mark yanked at his wrist ties so hard that he lifted the chair off the ground. Blue came round and put his thick hands on Mark's shoulders. Pushed down.

Grey took another step towards Nathan.

'We weren't going to hurt your daddy,' he said, inching forward.

'Stay away from me.' Nathan's eyes were wet as he shifted his weight from one bare foot to the other.

Mark wondered if the boy knew how to fire the gun.

191

Grey moved closer to Nathan.

'Leave him!' Mark said.

Blue held Mark's shoulders.

Grey took another step. His right hand was out, placating, his left hand holding the knife by his side. He was about three feet away from Nathan.

'Put your little gun down and come here,' he said.

Another step.

Mark struggled under the weight of Blue's grip.

Nathan closed his eyes and squeezed the trigger.

Nothing happened.

He opened his eyes and stared at the gun.

Grey laughed and took another step forward. He was almost at the boy now.

Nathan examined the gun, trembling. He looked at the side. Fumbled a sliding switch over. Squeezed the trigger.

The explosion was deafening. Grey and Nathan were lifted off their feet away from each other, the man slumping in the middle of the room, Nathan thudding against the wall next to the door.

Grey had dropped the knife. Blood pumped out of a large wound in his neck, and he was missing two fingers on his right hand, a mess of gore spread across his palm. He dragged his other hand to his neck but it was useless, blood poured everywhere, a chunk of his neck gone, his body twitching in shock.

Nathan sat against the wall with his eyes shut, gun still gripped in both his hands.

The stench of gunpowder haunted the room.

'Nathan!'

The boy opened his eyes, took a second to focus. He looked

at Grey on the ground, who had stopped twitching but was still breathing.

'Don't look at him,' Mark said.

Nathan turned to Mark. Then looked behind him. Mark realised that Blue's hands weren't on his shoulders any more. He swung his head round. Blue was edging towards the door.

Nathan lifted the gun and pointed it at him.

Blue broke into a run and flew towards the door. Mark heard him stumbling out the front door and down the stairwell, the bottom door slamming.

Mark looked at Nathan. The gun was limp in his hands, and he was staring at Grey on the floor. Blood pooled underneath the man's head and spread out, running along the grooves between the floorboards.

Mark tried to think. 'I said don't look at him.'

Nathan didn't move.

'Nathan. Look at Daddy.'

The boy slowly turned his head towards Mark.

'Now listen carefully. Daddy needs your help. Can you help me?'

His voice had reverted to toddler level, simple instructions and questions, referring to himself in the third person. Easier to get through to the boy.

Nathan nodded, a tiny head wobble.

'OK, good boy. Now come over here to me.'

Nathan dropped the gun and pushed himself up against the wall.

'That's it.' Mark's voice becoming more normal as Nathan responded.

Nathan did a zombie shuffle over to Mark, looking at the bleeding man the whole time.

'No, don't look at him, look at me.'

Nathan turned. He was at Mark now. Mark wished he could put his arms around the boy, shelter him from all of this.

'Now, listen to me, Nathan. Are you listening?'

A nod.

'Good. Daddy's hands are tied to this chair. I need you to un-tie me, OK?'

Another nod.

'OK?'

'OK.' The first word he'd spoken since the shooting.

'Good, now look at the knot behind my back, can you see how to undo it?'

Nathan moved behind the chair and Mark felt him make little tugs on the cable. The boy couldn't tie shoelaces, he'd never had to, kids' shoes were all Velcro these days. He didn't have any experience of trying to untie knots.

'Can you see a bit you could pull at to make it come loose?'

'I don't know.'

Just then Grey let out a groan that made them both jump. More like a moaning beast than anything human. Nathan backed away from the knot at Mark's wrists. Mark tried to keep his voice level.

'Nathan, I really need you to do this. Can you do it?'

'I don't know.'

'Just try. Pull on one of the bits of cable that looks like it might come loose.'

Grey groaned again. 'Fuck,' he said.

Then he moved.

He rolled over a little and waved his dismembered hand in the air.

'Fuck.'

'Daddy.' Nathan had a tremor in his voice.

'It's OK,' Mark said. 'Just ignore him. He can't hurt us any more. Concentrate on Daddy's wrists, OK?'

Mark felt Nathan tugging at the cable and he flexed his hands, trying to create leverage. Nothing yet.

'That's it, you're doing great. Keep going.' Mark put on his happiest, most encouraging voice. The one used for homework sessions and taking medicine.

Grey let his injured hand fall to the floor and yelled. Nathan and Mark jumped.

'Shit,' Grey said. 'Fuck.'

Mark wondered how he could speak with half his throat missing. Grey's left hand was still at his neck, soaked in blood, the hoodie fabric glistening and discoloured.

Grey rolled over on to his side and opened his eyes. Looked at Mark and Nathan.

'Come on,' Mark said. 'The knot. Pull it.'

'Daddy?' It sounded like Nathan needed to piss, agitated.

'Just do it.' All calmness gone from Mark's voice now.

Grey looked around, dazed. Mark wondered if he could see properly. Then Grey spotted the gun over by the door. Propped himself up on his elbow, hand still at his throat. The movement made more blood pour out the wound.

Mark couldn't feel anything happening behind him. 'Nathan? Come on.'

'I'm scared, Daddy.'

'I know, just concentrate. Try to untie the knot. Quickly.'

More tugging. Mark squirmed his hands around, trying to loosen things off. He bent his hands back, examining the tangle of cable with his own fingers as best he could. 'This bit I'm touching, try pulling this bit out.'

He felt Nathan's fingers pulling at it.

Grey began dragging himself across the floor. 'Jesus fucking ... shit ... Christ fuck ...' He wheezed out the words between coughs and cries of pain. He tried to get to his knees but crumpled. Pulled himself along using his maimed hand, thick smears of blood left in his wake. He was moving towards the gun.

'Nathan?'

'I'm trying.'

Grey was halfway to the gun. Mark felt Nathan pulling hard at the cable knot. Had something loosened?

'Never mind that,' Mark said. 'Change of plan. Go and get the gun.'

'What?'

'Get the gun and bring it over here.'

'Daddy...'

'Just get it.'

Grey was a few feet from the gun now.

'Quickly!'

Nathan scurried across the room.

'Stay away from the man.'

Too late.

Nathan was running past him when Grey lunged forward and grabbed the boy's ankle with his bleeding hand. Nathan tumbled like in a rugby tackle, just short of the gun, thumping into the floor with a sickening noise.

'Nathan!' Mark wrenched his hands behind his back and felt the cable slacken a little.

Grey held on to Nathan's ankle and began pulling. Nathan squirmed and kicked. Grey was heaving with the effort of holding on, Nathan letting out strangled gasps as he tried to break free.

Mark finally found the loose link in the knot and started unravelling it, his fingers fumbling.

Grey pulled Nathan towards him, blood everywhere, soaking into the bottom of the boy's jammies, smudged all over his ankle and foot. Nathan kicked at Grey's arm with his other foot, but somehow the man held on with only three fingers.

Mark almost had his hands free. Something was snagging though, a last loop of the cable stuck around part of the chair. He yanked at it.

Grey took his hand away from his neck and grabbed Nathan's leg with it, dragging the boy closer, clawing up his leg.

Nathan kicked out with his other foot, the same move he'd used earlier on Mark, the legbreaker. He brought his heel down hard on Grey's neck.

Grey screamed and fell back, letting go of Nathan's leg and clutching at his neck with both hands.

Nathan slithered backwards through the mess of blood to the doorway and the gun.

Mark felt his hands release and sprang out of the chair. He bolted over to Grey and kicked him hard, then collected Nathan in his arms and picked up the Browning.

'It's OK.' He clutched Nathan and stroked his hair. 'It's OK. Daddy's here.'

They both heaved air into their lungs as they watched Grey

on the floor. He wasn't moving, just lying there on his back with his eyes closed, holding his neck.

Mark ushered Nathan out the door then crouched at his eye level, still with Grey in their line of sight. Grey didn't move.

'Listen to me,' Mark said. 'Look at me and listen.'

Nathan turned. Mark felt his heart tense at the look in Nathan's eyes. This would be with him forever. What kind of a parent was he, exposing his son to this?

'You've done nothing wrong,' Mark said. 'OK?'

Nathan just stared.

'Do you hear me?'

Nathan nodded, but it wasn't convincing.

'I'm going to deal with this. Go into Mummy and Daddy's bedroom and wait for me.'

Nathan hesitated.

Mark gave him a big hug. Felt the Browning in his hand against the small of the boy's back.

'I promise this will all be over soon. But you need to do as I say, OK?'

'OK.'

'Good. Now go and wait in the other room and I'll be through in a minute.'

'I don't want to leave you, Daddy.'

'No one's leaving anyone, Big Guy. I'm right here. Go and wait, I'll be with you in a second.'

Nathan turned and scuffed to the bedroom. Mark watched him go, smiling falsely when the boy turned back to look at him.

34

The man hadn't moved. Blood everywhere, a pool of it in the middle of the floor, rivulets running off in different directions, smears from the pool to the door.

Mark stood looking at him. The man's chest was rising and falling in a shallow, uneven lurch. Still alive, then. Hands at his throat, eyes closed. He still had the dust mask on.

Mark thought.

His son had shot someone. With an illegal gun. But Nathan had been protecting his daddy. The men had broken in.

He checked the Browning. Safety off.

He crept towards the man on the floor. Gave him a tentative kick in the ribs. Grey let out a soft groan. Looked like he was concentrating on staying alive.

Mark squatted down on his haunches next to the man's head. Blood was still oozing through the fingers at his neck, dripping from the stumps on his hand. So Nathan's bullet had taken two fingers off his outstretched hand then ploughed into his neck. Good shot, Big Guy.

Mark nudged at Grey's temple with the gun barrel.

'Hey.'

The man's breathing got louder, but that was it.

'Look at me.'

A few seconds, then his eyelids fluttered open. Mark wanted

to see something in those eyes, like you read in books. That he was evil, or scared, or sorry. Anything. But it didn't work like that. They were just a man's empty eyes.

Mark reached out and pulled the dust mask down from Grey's face. The nose had been broken in the past, the mouth small, cluttered with brown teeth. The smell of hash and whisky mingled with the ferric tang of blood.

'Can you speak?'

The man's eyes moved to look at Mark.

'Who do you work for?'

He blinked, made the slightest sideways motion with his head. Like Nathan when he didn't want to admit he'd done something naughty.

Mark shook his head. 'That's not very clever.'

Grey coughed and blood spattered out his mouth, leaving a thin dribble down his chin.

Mark sucked his teeth. 'I could phone an ambulance.'

The man's eyes widened.

'Then again, I might not.'

Grey just breathed. Ragged. In. Out.

'Looks like you could do with one.'

Grey closed his eyes, like a long blink, then struggled to open them again. He took a while to focus.

'Come on,' Mark said. 'I'll make it easy for you.'

Another cough, more blood.

'This is about my wife, right?'

A wheezy, rasping breath.

'Who are you working for? Taylor?'

Nothing in his face gave anything away.

'Fisher?'

His eyes moved, avoided Mark's gaze.

'You work for Fisher?'

He kept his eyes turned away.

Mark moved the muzzle of the Browning from Grey's head and stuck it into his neck. He grunted in pain, rolled his head. That was all he could manage. He looked like he was about to die.

'Tell me you work for Fisher, or I'll make this pain so much worse.'

The man looked at Mark, then closed his eyes and nodded.

'Tell me.'

His lips parted. He coughed blood.

'Fisher.'

'Did he kill my wife?'

Slight shake of the head.

'Did you kill her?'

A more vigorous shake.

'Then who did?'

The man's eyes went to the door. Mark followed his gaze.

'The other guy?'

A clear nod.

Mark wondered about that.

'Is that the truth?'

A cough then a whisper. 'Yes.'

'Why?'

A slight shake of the head.

'Why was Lauren killed?'

Mark pushed the Browning further into his neck wound. Grey's body went rigid with pain and he spat blood.

'What password were you talking about?'

'Ambulance,' he said.

'No ambulance. Tell me first.'

'Ambulance.'

Mark pushed the gun further. Grey choked, then closed his eyes.

Mark slapped his cheek. Nothing. Slapped him again. Checked his pulse.

Unconscious. Fuck.

Mark stood up and backed away.

He left the room. Flicked the safety on the gun and tucked it into the back of his jeans.

Went into the bedroom.

Nathan was sitting on the bed, head slumped. The wardrobe door was still open, the underwear drawer pulled out. The empty shammy cloth on the bed.

Mark thought about the man dying next door.

And Fisher.

'Am I in trouble, Daddy?'

Mark sat down next to him and pulled him close, lifted his chin up. The look in Nathan's eyes made him catch his breath. So much to deal with, only six years old.

'No, you're not in trouble. You've been a very brave boy. Do you understand?'

'But I shot that man.'

'He was hurting Daddy, wasn't he? You helped me.'

Nathan reached out to Mark's neck. Where the tip of the knife had gone in. Mark laid his hand over the boy's and lifted it away. Both hands with bloody fingers. Mark dabbed at the wound. Didn't seem to still be bleeding, only a nick really.

'Is he a bad man?'

'Yes, a very bad man.'

'Is he dead? Did I kill him?'

'He's not dead, no.'

'Then shouldn't we get him some help?'

Mark tried to think straight. How would this play out? Should he call the police and tell the truth? He had to think about what would happen to Nathan. Maybe Mark should say that he shot the man. But then what would happen to him? Would Nathan be able to stick to a lie? He was terrible at lying at the best of times, but maybe Mark just thought that because he knew the boy so well, knew when he wasn't telling the truth. No, a six-year-old wouldn't hold up under police interrogation, no way. Then they would just be in even deeper shit.

They should keep Grey alive so he could link Fisher to everything. What was the link, though? Anyway, once Grey got better, he might change his story, deny all knowledge, just make out it was a simple break-in.

Mark rubbed Nathan's shoulders.

'Wait here.'

'Don't leave me, Daddy.'

'I'm just going to check on the bad man, OK? I'll be back in a few seconds.'

He walked through the flat and into the living room. His stomach lurched when he saw the mess again. Grey was still there in the middle of it, hadn't moved.

Mark stared at the body. No movement. He walked across and crouched over the man. Laid a hand on his chest. Nothing. Put his hand over Grey's mouth. Didn't feel any breath. Took hold of the guy's wrist and felt with his forefinger and thumb. Held him like that for a while.

No pulse.

Too late for an ambulance.

He couldn't link Fisher and Taylor to Lauren's murder now.

Mark saw his possible futures disappearing, paths vanishing in fog. He tried to see a way clear, but couldn't.

'Daddy?'

Mark turned.

Nathan was standing in the doorway, staring at the body.

'Should we get an ambulance for him?'

Mark ran a hand through his hair and went over to the boy. Tried to turn him away from the corpse, but met resistance. Nathan was transfixed.

'Look at me,' Mark said.

Nathan turned slowly. 'He's dead, isn't he?' The boy's eyes filled with tears. 'I killed him.'

Mark pulled him into a hug. Tried to imagine what was going through his mind. What could he possibly tell him that would make this go away? Nothing. That was the truth of it. Nothing could undo this.

'I already told you, Big Guy, you didn't do anything wrong.'

'But I killed that man.'

'You had to. It's called self-defence. Do you know what that is?'

A slight shake of the head amongst the sniffles and tears.

Mark lifted Nathan's chin up again. 'It's when you have to stop someone from hurting you or hurting someone you love. You have to do it, you don't have any choice.'

Nathan frowned and stole a glance at the corpse again.

'It means it wasn't your fault.'

Nathan's breath was ragged as his chest heaved. 'So I won't get into trouble with the police?'

Mark shook his head, a dumb, exaggerated movement. 'I promise, you won't get in any trouble with the police.'

He tried to think about that. He wished it was that simple. His mind was scrambled, he couldn't think straight. He wanted to reassure the boy some more, say something that would make a difference. But what the hell could he say?

'Should we call the police now, Daddy? Tell them what's happened.'

Mark frowned. He needed time to work things out.

'Not yet, Big Guy.'

He gave Nathan another big, long cuddle, then stood up. Went to the sofa and picked up his phone. Pressed a number and waited till he heard a familiar voice.

'We need help.'

35

'Where's my grandson?'

Mark nodded towards the bedroom door.

Ruth scuttled in and brushed past him. He trailed behind her.

Nathan was under the covers, staring at the ceiling. Ruth gave him a suffocating hug.

As he watched them, Mark realised he still had the gun stuck down the back of his jeans. He pulled his T-shirt down to cover it.

He'd explained to Ruth over the phone some of what had happened. She came straight away. He hadn't called anyone else. No point in an ambulance, and he wasn't sure about the police, not yet.

No one else had come round either, no police or neighbours. He wondered about that, with the gunshot noise, but he could understand people wanting to keep out of trouble.

While he'd waited for Ruth to arrive, he'd washed the blood off Nathan's legs and feet then washed the boy's hands thoroughly. Thought about gunpowder residue. Then got a change of jammies and threw the dirty ones in the washing machine. Pointless really, with a corpse leaking pints of blood all over the living room, but the methodical, mundane appearance of housework kept his mind from caving in. Nathan was like a zombie again, doing exactly what he was told, blank look on his face. Mark felt a rock in his stomach as he saw that look. He tried to think about the boy's mind, about how this was all piling up on top of them, but his own brain couldn't cope with it. They had both been reduced to basic functioning to keep their sanity and their lives together.

He was chewing it all up again as Ruth fussed over Nathan in bed now.

Fisher.

Fisher was responsible, but he had no proof, just a dead man's word for it. He'd gone through the man's pockets, no ID. Would the police take Mark seriously? Ferguson had already ignored him when he mentioned Fisher and Taylor. Mark had an assault charge pending thanks to that school thing, and now he had a dead man in his living room. That his son had shot and killed.

Ruth got up from the bed and turned to Mark.

'Where's the . . .'

Mark nodded towards the living room then followed as she went through.

Ruth put her hands to her mouth. 'Mother of God.' She crossed herself.

He tried to see it through her eyes. It was a fucking mess, a bloody, violent, disgusting mess. And he was responsible, he was in charge and had exposed her grandchild to this.

Ruth turned away from the body. 'Have you phoned the police?'

'Not yet.'

'Why not?'

'I'm not sure.'

'What will happen to Nathan?'

'I don't know.'

'Can they charge him with murder?'

'I don't know.'

Ruth stared at him. 'You don't know much, do you?'

Mark scratched at his scalp. 'I could say I did it.'

'Then you might get put away, leaving him with no parents at all. I don't think so.'

They stood looking at each other.

Ruth spoke. 'I could say I did it.'

Mark thought about that. Shook his head.

'Nathan would never be able to stick to a lie.'

'He could just say he was asleep the whole time.'

'And what were you doing round here?'

'Staying over to help out, since Lauren's . . .'

Mark put a hand on her shoulder. He could see she was serious.

'No. I think we have to tell the truth. For Nathan's sake as much as anything else.'

Ruth glanced back at the body. 'Why did he have to break in here of all places?'

Mark sighed. He hadn't told her on the phone.

'It wasn't random. He told me something.'

There was a slow spread of realisation on Ruth's face. 'This is to do with Lauren?'

Mark nodded and looked at the corpse. 'He worked for someone who knew Lauren's boss.'

'So?'

'I don't know, he didn't tell me. But it's not just a coincidence.

They were here looking for a password. But I've already checked all Lauren's online stuff, I didn't find anything.'

'We have to tell the police straight away.'

'No.'

'What do you mean, no?'

'This guy's dead, so I've got no link to Lauren.'

'Just tell the police what he told you.'

'Why would they believe me? I need to get some evidence.'

'No, you just need to tell the truth.'

Mark rubbed at his eye. 'No, I need evidence.'

He walked through to the bedroom, Ruth behind. Nathan was asleep.

They both stood staring at him.

Ruth sat down on the bed and laid a hand on the covers. Raised her other hand to her brow. 'This is all too much.' She waved her hand around. 'This is all just too much to take.'

'It'll soon be over,' Mark said.

He got Ferguson's card from his pocket and held it out to her.

'Phone this number and tell her everything that's happened.'

Ruth hesitated then eventually took the card.

'Everything?'

Mark nodded. 'There's no point trying to cover it up.'

Ruth stared at the card. 'What are you going to do?'

Mark looked at Nathan and thought about Lauren.

'I'm going to get some evidence.'

36

As he drove through empty streets, he could feel fury simmer inside him, replacing the adrenalin from the break-in. He nurtured it, built it into something he could use for what was coming.

And yet he was still plagued by doubt. What did Lauren and Caledonia Dreaming have to do with this guy Fisher, someone who could hire thugs to burgle and torture people? What was the password they wanted? What would the police do once they got to the flat? Was he right to leave Ruth to look after Nathan and deal with all that? They'd be safer in police custody than where he was going.

The thought of Nathan made his stomach cramp. His son had killed a man to save his daddy. What a thing to live with for the rest of your life. On top of Lauren dying and everything else, this was a lifetime of trauma piling up.

The wind was still tormenting the trees as he sped round Cameron Toll towards Morningside and Merchiston. Taxis and night buses trundled along the street as he raced across roundabouts and junctions.

He drove past all the big houses with sprawling gardens, moneyed families sleeping soundly at night, never any problems in their little bubble worlds.

He shot across Holy Corner and hung a right, slowing, trying to keep his hands on the wheel from shaking.

He stopped a few doors down from number 40. There were no cars parked on the street, everyone in their driveways, so he stuck out as a stranger, an unwelcome intrusion on the leafy paradise. Fuck it.

He glanced down at the pistol on the passenger seat. One fired round meant nine bullets left. He hoped he didn't have to rely on that knowledge.

He picked it up, ejected the magazine, counted the bullets to be sure, then pushed it back in. Kept the safety on for now. Hauled open the car door and tucked the gun into his jeans.

The wind was making a racket in the tops of the oaks lining the street.

He got to number 40. The metal gates were closed across the entrance to the driveway, a hefty lock with a buzzer system.

Mark stepped back and scoped the place. He spotted a CCTV camera and ducked in behind the pillar. The gates were ten feet tall topped with iron spikes. The old stone wall to the side was shorter, but the top of it was coated in a line of cement with bits of broken glass jutting out. Mark had seen similar on houses across Edinburgh. Old homemade defences.

He looked at the camera. It was stationary, pointing at the middle of the gates. He didn't think it could see him from here. He crouched then leapt, got a hand on the top of the wall, but jerked it away as a piece of glass sliced into his palm.

'Shit.'

He looked at his hand. Just a shallow cut, nothing serious. He pulled his jacket sleeve down over his fist then jumped again, this time finding a hold in between the bits of glass. He kicked at a part of the stone wall and a small crumble of masonry fell out. He chipped away with his foot at the dried mortar until he had a foothold, then hoisted himself up, grabbing the top of the pillar with his other hand.

He heaved with both arms and dragged his body to the top of the wall, his stomach snagging on the glass embedded there. He sucked his gut in as the glass scraped at his T-shirt. He hovered for a moment, supported only by his hands, then carefully placed a knee on the wall between glass shards. Then on to his feet. The drop at the other side was less, only five feet to a landscaped lawn.

He jumped and crouched on landing, then was up and jogging towards the house. It was a mansion really. There were six cars parked in the driveway, room for several more. They were all out of sight from the main road. Mark wondered about that. He hunched and ran alongside the cars, then stopped at one. A silver Lexus. Mark knew the number plate from staring at it as he followed it across town.

Taylor.

He approached the front door. No light on over the porch. As he got nearer he noticed that all the windows had blackout blinds. He scanned upstairs. It looked the same, as far as he could tell from down here.

He walked round the house. All the windows were blacked out. What the hell was going on inside?

Round the back he heard voices. He pulled the Browning from his jeans and flicked the safety off. Ducked into the shadows of the house, pushed himself against the stonework and poked his head out.

There was a conservatory built out from the back of the house. The only piece of glasswork in the whole building you could see into. Two huge men in black bomber jackets were smoking at an open patio door. Serious bouncers. But bouncers for what?

He couldn't make out what they were saying. They finished their cigarettes, spat on the gravel, then went inside and slid the door closed. He didn't know if they'd locked it or not. They left the conservatory and sauntered back into the house.

He crept to the door, keeping an eye on the inside. Didn't see anyone. He tried the handle. Locked. Looked around for something heavy. Nothing.

He flicked the safety on the gun, wrapped it in the material of his jacket pocket, then thumped it at a corner of the glass.

The smash echoed in his ears.

He held his breath and waited.

No one came.

He reached in with his hand covered in his sleeve and slid the lock over. Pulled the door open and went inside. He felt drawn into the building, as if he had no free will any more. He had to let this happen, had to find out.

He crept from the conservatory into a utility room. Washing machine and dishwasher, food cupboards. From there through to a hallway. It was dark, but light spilled from a big room at the front of the house. He heard voices and laughter. Men. A clinking of glasses and bottles.

He crouched, scared to go closer. Just then, a man came from the room into the hall. Mark ducked back into the utility room and peeked round. The man stopped halfway down the hall and went into a bathroom.

Then another man came out the room, this time with a woman in her underwear. She was black, strong features, high heels and white lace. He was in a grey suit. They were arm in arm as they headed up the stairs.

A brothel.

The other man came out the toilet and went back into the lit room.

Mark waited. Didn't know what to do. Couldn't think straight. He stayed there, his pulse thumping, his breath shallow and fast. He thought about Lauren. He gripped the gun handle tighter. Stepped from the utility room. Heard voices again, coming from upstairs. Getting louder. He ducked back inside.

A man and a woman. He recognised the man's voice, then saw him coming down the stairs.

Taylor. With another prostitute, blonde, Eastern European-looking, in a kimono. They both went into the main downstairs room and Mark heard other voices, it sounded like guys taking the piss out of each other, or sharing a joke.

Mark realised he'd been holding his breath, and puffed air out of his lungs.

What was the link to Lauren?

As he stood there wondering, another couple came out the room and headed upstairs – him a fat, middle-aged guy in a black suit, her a beautiful redhead, tall and sleek.

Then Taylor appeared again, this time heading for the front door with one of the bouncers. He buttoned up his suit then put a hand on the bouncer's shoulder and handed him some money.

Mark scurried through the utility room to the conservatory and slipped out. Darted round the side of the house and stood in a small copse of elm that was shimmering in the wind. He watched Taylor come down the steps waving to the bouncer, then he was in darkness as the front door closed.

Mark moved through the trees until he was as close as he could get to the Lexus.

Taylor was almost at the car now, his key out, the security lights on the Lexus blinking as he unlocked it. In the flashing amber, he was grinning, smug.

Mark stepped away from the trees and strode towards him, pointing the Browning.

'Don't make a fucking sound.'

Taylor stopped. He looked as if he'd been punched in the gut. He turned to the house.

'Don't even think about it.'

Taylor's eyes darted around.

'I will shoot you. Don't think I won't.'

Taylor seemed to deflate a little.

'Now get in the car.'

Taylor just stood there looking at Mark.

'I said, get in.'

Taylor slowly opened the driver's door and got in. Mark kept the gun on him and got into the back seat.

Taylor turned round. 'Look . . .'

Mark brought the butt of the gun down on the side of his face.

'Fuck.' Taylor grabbed at his eyebrow. It swelled up straight away, his eye closing a little. 'Jesus Christ.'

He clutched at his forehead and breathed out heavily.

Mark pressed the gun to his neck.

'Tell me what the fuck is going on here.'

Taylor leaned away from the gun barrel pressed against the flesh of his neck. Mark jabbed it in again.

Taylor flinched. 'OK, take it easy.'

He seemed too calm, Mark didn't like it.

Mark flicked his head towards the house. 'Is Fisher in there?'

'I don't know anyone called Fisher.'

Mark drew the gun back and smashed the butt into Taylor's face, at the swollen bit. This time the skin broke and blood spurted out so far it splattered on the inside of the windscreen.

'Shit.' Taylor clutched at his eye. He hunched forward for a moment. 'You'll fucking blind me.'

'I'll do worse than that if you don't tell me what I need to know.'

Taylor gasped in air and sniffed, wiped blood away from his eye, but still didn't speak.

'Is Fisher in there?' Mark said.

Taylor glanced at the house, Mark followed his gaze. No sign of activity.

'How do you know about Fisher?'

'I saw you meet him. I followed him here.'

Taylor shook his head. 'You have no idea what you're getting into.'

'Is he in there?'

Taylor dabbed at his eye. His hand came away bloody. 'No.'

'Does he own the brothel?'

Taylor laughed, then nodded.

'What's all this got to do with Lauren?'

Taylor's leg was twitching. 'What do you mean?'

'Don't fuck around. Tell me.'

'It doesn't have anything to do with Lauren.'

Mark grabbed his hair and pulled his head back. He jammed the Browning under Taylor's jaw, pointing up.

'Look, I've got a dead guy bleeding all over my living-room floor. Him and another guy came to my flat while me and my son were asleep, tied me to a chair and beat me. Told me they were looking for a password and were working for Fisher. So why don't you tell me how this is connected before I blow your fucking head all across this beautiful interior.'

He wondered if he could really do it.

Taylor gave him a deadpan look. Almost a smile. 'I don't know anything about all that.'

Mark pushed the muzzle of the pistol into Taylor's left shoulder and pulled the trigger.

The blast of the gun was deafening in the car. Blood sprayed from the wound over the gun, Mark's hand and the windscreen. Taylor rocked in his seat then lunged forward in pain. The back of his shoulder was a ragged hole, the bullet had made a mess coming out. Blood pulsed out the hole in Taylor's suit as he screamed and clutched at his shoulder.

Mark grabbed his hair and yanked him back into his seat, then jammed the Browning against his head.

The smell of gunpowder hung in the air. Behind it, Mark thought he caught a whiff of piss. Taylor must've wet himself.

Mark looked at the house. Nothing.

He turned back to Taylor. 'Tell me what this has to do with Lauren.'

'You don't understand. He'll kill me.'

Mark moved the Browning from Taylor's head to his knee.

'Maybe you want to be in a fucking wheelchair for the rest of your life?'

Taylor looked scared now. Good. His hand was at his bleeding shoulder, his eyes looking at the gun pressed against his kneecap.

'It wasn't my fault,' he said. 'I didn't know what Fisher had planned. It was only supposed to be a warning, that's what he told me.'

Mark glanced behind him at the house. Still in darkness.

'Go on.'

Taylor was trembling, almost crying.

'Fisher has lots of places like this. Caledonia Dreaming helps him find the properties. He finds the girls.'

Mark thought about what he'd seen inside.

'Trafficking?'

Taylor nodded stiffly.

'What else?'

Taylor shook his head and cringed.

'Are you stupid?' Mark said, pressing the barrel of the Browning into Taylor's knee. 'I will shoot your fucking kneecap clean off.'

Taylor looked at the gun, then at his bloody shoulder. 'He uses Caledonia Dreaming to clean his money.'

'Laundering.'

'He buys legitimate properties with the profits and sells them on.'

Mark was starting to see. 'Lauren found out.'

'Yes.'

'And you had her killed.'

Taylor smelled of panic now. 'It wasn't like that. Lauren came to me with information. It didn't occur to her that I was involved. She'd been looking at accounts she shouldn't have. Her being a junior partner, she felt she had a lot to lose if the company was into dodgy shit. I stalled her, told her I'd take it to the police. Then I told Fisher. He was supposed to warn her off. I could never approve of murder.'

Mark lifted the gun and smacked it off Taylor's face again, this time the cheekbone. He heard a crack.

'Couldn't fucking approve? Prostitution, trafficking and money-laundering are fine, though, yeah?'

'I liked Lauren, she was a good friend.'

'I swear, don't you dare insult her memory like that or I will shoot you in the fucking face.'

The gun was rammed into Taylor's damaged cheek now.

Mark thought of his wife's dry lips, her tangle of hair.

'So these guys at my flat were after a password.'

Taylor nodded.

'What password?'

Taylor took his hand away from his shoulder and flinched. 'Fuck, this hurts.'

'Just tell me.'

'Are you going to take me to a hospital?'

'Just tell me.'

Taylor hesitated, then gave him a resigned look. 'We checked her work email. She sent a copy of the files to her Gmail account.'

Mark sighed. Remembered the Excel spreadsheets he'd opened and disregarded that first night. Then remembered being at Taylor's office. 'And I told you I knew the password.'

Taylor nodded.

Mark rubbed at his forehead. 'Where's Fisher now?'

'I don't know. He only usually comes here during the day.'

Mark thought about that.

'OK, we're going to the police.'

'I need to go to hospital.'

'Police first, then hospital.'

Taylor looked at his shoulder. 'I don't think I can drive.'

'Try.'

Taylor just sat there. Mark jabbed the butt of the gun into his face again, at the broken cheek. Taylor let out a yelp.

'OK, OK.'

He started the engine and pushed the parking brake off. Then leaned over, breathing heavily, and stuck the car into gear with his right hand. Sat back and grimaced.

'You're going to tell the cops everything you just told me,' Mark said.

Taylor was shaking. He stank of piss and blood. 'Fisher will kill me if I do that.'

Mark stared at him.

'I'll kill you if you don't.'

37

Taylor drove east, struggling with the gears.

Mark kept the gun stubbed into the side of his skull. He wondered about Taylor's injuries. Confession under duress. Mark could get charged with armed assault or maybe attempted murder. He tried not to think about that. Or about the repercussions of Nathan shooting the man at the flat. But for all that, the police was surely the right way to go. Any attempt to cover this up would just come back to bite them.

He presumed Ruth and Nathan were at the police station already. He phoned Ruth's mobile. No answer.

He called Portobello Police Station. It went straight on to voicemail. Either the guy on the front desk was asleep or he was speaking to someone, or there was no one at reception. How could there be no answer from a police station? Manpower cuts?

He called the flat, just in case. No reply.

Then he called Ferguson. Voicemail.

He tried Ruth again. No answer.

Fuck.

Mark watched the blur of streetlights outside. Checked the clock in the car. 3.15 a.m.

'Slight change of plan,' he said. 'We're dropping in to my flat first.'

'No way,' Taylor said, crunching the gearbox. 'I need medical attention.'

Mark tapped the Browning's muzzle against his temple.

'Just drive.'

They drove for a while in silence, then Taylor spoke. 'Fisher is going to kill both of us.'

Mark thrust the Browning into Taylor's neck. 'He won't get a chance, the police will arrest him.'

Taylor laughed, not a happy sound. 'You don't understand, he's a psycho and he's well connected. He'll still get to us.'

Mark examined his cut hand. It was scabbing over already. 'How did you get involved with him in the first place?'

Taylor didn't answer.

'Fine,' Mark said. 'I don't give a shit. It doesn't matter.'

Taylor sighed. 'School, believe it or not. Heriot's.'

'The pair of you went to Heriot's?'

Taylor nodded stiffly. 'He was a bully. I was glad to see the back of him. Lost contact for years. Then one day he turned up in the office and I didn't have any choice.'

'You had a choice. We all have choices.'

'Do you have a choice just now?'

Mark thought about that. He flicked his head back the way they'd come.

'You seemed to be enjoying yourself back there. I wonder what your wife and kids would think of that.'

They drove on in silence again before Taylor spoke.

'Fisher will do anything to protect his interests.'

'Me too.'

Mark looked out the window as a taxi chugged in the opposite direction. They skirted round the back of Arthur's Seat, the side the tourists never see. Just a looming presence in the darkness, an absence of stars.

'How big is this whole thing?'

Taylor swallowed but stayed silent.

'You might as well tell me,' Mark said. 'You're fucked now anyway.'

Taylor winced as he changed gear again. 'It's worth millions.'

'And the police don't have a clue?'

Taylor laughed. 'Half the police force use Fisher's places, it's not in their interests to shut him down. And no one's ever been done for trafficking or laundering in this country.'

Mark stared at Taylor. 'How do you square it with yourself, being a part of all this?'

Taylor shrugged. 'I did what I had to do to protect my family. Just like you're trying to do.'

'And how does that fit with sleeping with trafficked prostitutes?'

They hit a stretch of speed bumps in Duddingston, then the cobbles of Brighton Place slowed them down. Not a single person on the streets out here in the suburbs, the same as they turned along Porty High Street.

Mark felt his stomach tense up as they neared the flat.

As if sensing something, Taylor spoke.

'You're fucked, you know, you're way out of your depth.'

38

'Pull in here.'

Taylor squeezed in across the road from the flat, right next to the church. Bumped on to the kerb like every other car.

The wind was hurtling up Marlborough Street from the sea, bustling the Lexus. Taylor killed the engine and slumped back into his seat holding his shoulder. His face was ashen.

The car groaned and squeaked with the gusts of wind. Mark looked up at the windows of the flat. The living-room light was on, curtains closed. Same with the bedroom. He tried to remember how they'd been when he left, but couldn't.

He shuffled sideways in his seat but kept the gun on Taylor. 'Out the car.'

Taylor climbed out, leaving a sodden mess of blood on the upholstery, then Mark slid out the car after him.

'Come on.'

Mark walked with Taylor in front, gun pressed into his back.

'There's no need for that,' Taylor said.

'Just move.'

The bottom door was closed. He unlocked it and pushed Taylor forward by the crook of his good arm.

He shushed Taylor. Listened. Nothing but the buzz of the striplight in the stairwell.

They walked up the spiral staircase.

The door to the flat was closed but the catch on the lock was hanging off. Still like that from the first break-in.

Mark kept the gun pointing at Taylor and touched the door open.

He didn't know whether to speak out or not. Nathan and Ruth were probably at the police station, right? He just wanted to make sure.

Mark was standing in the doorway, Taylor beside him, when the door flew open then back at him with force, the wood smashing off his skull and throwing him off balance.

The gun was knocked from his hand, then the door opened and closed again, someone heavy behind it, and Mark's arm and chest were crushed between the door and the frame, squeezing the breath out of him. He felt his legs crumple as he stuck his head round the door to see who was there. He saw a flash of light as a heavy torch swung down and connected with his cheek and mouth, splitting his lip.

He fell to the floor and took another blow, this time to the side of his head, then he felt two kicks to his ribs and he lost all balance and sprawled out in the hallway, struggling to gasp air into his lungs.

He scrambled around feeling for the pistol he'd dropped, then a boot stamped on his fingers. He yowled and yanked his hand into his armpit.

He was dragged by his legs to the living room, kicking feebly out, then he was flung into the middle of the room, followed by a couple more boots to his lower back, his kidneys taking the brunt.

He struggled to breathe. Tried to focus. The room was bright, the light on overhead. The stench of blood, shit and piss filled his nostrils. Also something else. Cologne. Expensive cologne.

'Hello, Mark.'

A man's voice. Controlled. Mark hadn't heard the voice before but he knew who it was and his skin crawled.

He struggled on to his knees and looked up.

Fisher was sitting in the same chair Mark had been tied up in, hands on his lap.

The dead man was still lying on the floor nearby, the spread of blood reaching out all around him.

'Daddy.'

He turned. Nathan and Ruth were on the sofa. Both had been crying. Ruth's face was red, like she'd been hit. Nathan was still in his replacement jammies, another pair that were too small for him. His bare feet pulled up under him looked so vulnerable and frail. Confusion and fear on his face. Mark cursed himself for ever leaving the flat.

He shuffled over to the sofa and scooped Nathan into his arms. Held him tight against his chest and felt the boy shake.

'I'm sorry,' he whispered in the boy's ear.

Fisher spoke. 'This is such a mess.'

Mark turned. Taylor and the guy in the blue hoodie who had run away earlier were standing at the door of the room. Blue had a torch in one hand and Mark's pistol in the other. It had been so easy.

Mark was stupid, stupid, stupid.

But he was thinking. Thinking how he could get Nathan and Ruth out of this. Calculating his odds if he rushed one of them, if he managed to grapple the gun from Blue.

Fisher's eyebrows rose when he saw Taylor's shoulder and

face. He smiled and shook his head. He turned to Mark. 'You caught up with Gavin, then. I want you to know, this is not what we do.'

Mark stared at him. 'Kill people?'

'Precisely.'

'You prefer human trafficking.'

Fisher frowned at Taylor and sucked his teeth. 'All my girls work voluntarily. They are paid very well for what they do. And they don't have to work on the streets, with dangerous, violent punters who rape and beat them. We only deal with the best patrons.'

'Let us go,' Mark said.

'I wish I could.'

Taylor stepped forward into the room, hand on shoulder. 'I need to get to a hospital.'

Fisher turned and pulled a gun out of his coat pocket and pointed it at Taylor.

'Actually, this is all your fault.'

Taylor put a hand out towards Fisher. 'Wait a minute.'

'If you'd been more careful at Caledonia Dreaming, none of this would've happened.'

Taylor shook his head. 'I didn't kill Lauren.'

Mark bristled at the mention of her name.

Taylor continued. 'There wasn't supposed to be any killing.'

Fisher glanced at Blue. 'That was a mistake.'

Mark remembered what the dead man had said. That his partner had killed Lauren. Not exactly a reliable witness. But still.

Fisher sighed. 'And now we have all this.' He waved the gun around, at the dead man, at the three of them on the sofa.

Mark caught Ruth's eye. Couldn't work out what she was thinking. Probably hating him for letting her daughter get killed and getting her grandson into this unholy mess. He couldn't blame her.

Mark turned. He had Nathan in his grasp and he was five feet from the living-room door. Then another ten feet down the hallway to the front door. Fisher and Blue had guns. Taylor was in between them. Blue was pointing the Browning at Mark, while Fisher waved his gun around.

Mark wondered.

Then the buzzer went.

Everyone flinched.

Fisher got up and went to the window. Peeked out the side of a curtain. Looked back in the room and shrugged.

The buzzer went again.

Fisher looked at the clock on the mantelpiece. Twenty to four in the morning. He waved the gun at Blue to head towards the front door.

'Should I answer it?' Blue said.

'No. Just get behind the door.'

Blue went out to the hall.

The buzzer went a third time, longer, more persistent.

Mark could feel a chance coming. He was at the edge of his nerves, but he was ready, he felt ready. His body ached where it had taken a beating, but he drew energy from Nathan's touch, from the boy's heartbeat through his jammy top.

The flat was silent. All listening.

Footsteps up the stairwell. Mark must've left the bottom door open.

How many people? Mark couldn't tell.

He kept his eyes on Fisher, who was creeping forward, looking at the hallway, watching Blue behind the door. Blue had
his torch raised, shoulder prepped for slamming into whoever
came in, same as he'd done to Mark.

Fisher's attention was on the hallway. That's where his gun
was pointing too. Mark stared at it. Taylor was also watching
the front door.

Mark listened for anything from the stairwell and kept his
eye on Fisher's gun.

A knock.

With the lock broken, the door swung open a little. Light
bled in from the stairwell. The door opened out the other way
from the living room, so Mark couldn't see who was there, just
Blue waiting, torch above his head.

'Hello?'

Ferguson.

'Mr Douglas?'

The door opened wider, Ferguson's shadow blocking the
light from the stairwell, the hallway thrown back into darkness.

Then she was in the doorway. Mark saw her head and neck
as she peered round.

Blue pushed his shoulder into the door, which rammed into
her, knocking her against the door jamb so that she dropped to
the floor.

But just as he was about to bring the torch down on to her
head, the door was flung open again, knocking him off balance.

Another cop.

It was the uniformed kid she'd been with last time, at the
doorway, flinging punches behind the door, landing a few on
Blue.

Mark looked at Fisher. He'd edged into the hallway and was wondering what to do. He didn't have a clear shot. Taylor had moved in the opposite direction, backing away from it all and further into the room until he stumbled over the corpse then righted himself.

Mark saw his chance.

He held Nathan's hand tight and flicked his head to Ruth, indicating the front door.

Then he got up and ran, hauling Nathan with him, Ruth close behind.

They were already out the room and into the hallway when he heard Taylor.

'Fisher.'

But Fisher didn't have time to turn. Mark brought his fist down on Fisher's hand, making him drop the gun, then threw a shoulder at him on the way past, enough to knock Fisher off balance so that he had to lunge at the wall with his hand.

Ferguson was struggling to her knees. The door was wide open now. Blue had the kid cop by the throat, but the kid was swinging a baton and as Mark got there, the baton connected with Blue's nose and his grip loosened.

Mark pushed Nathan ahead of him, turning to check Ruth was still behind.

The three of them scrambled over Ferguson crouched on the floor then tumbled out the flat and into the stairwell. They clattered down the stairs in a flurry of limbs.

'Get them.' Fisher's voice.

Mark grabbed the bottom door and heaved it open and the three of them spilled out into the night.

39

He pushed Ruth and Nathan down the street and ran after them.

The boy was fast, even in bare feet. He was up front.

Mark could hear Ruth puffing beside him.

They were heading towards the prom.

The crack of a gunshot made Mark flinch.

He ducked, glanced back, ran on.

Fisher and Blue, both with guns. A hundred yards behind.

He couldn't see if Ferguson was there, or the other officer.

He looked at the houses as they ran past. No lights on. He thought about ringing a doorbell, but by the time anyone came Fisher and Blue would be on them. Game over.

Nathan turned to look at him and Ruth.

'Don't look back,' Mark said.

He and Ruth were gaining on the boy. Nathan had energy, but his legs didn't have the reach. Mark could hear the boy's feet slapping on the pavement.

Another shot.

Jesus Christ.

Mark zigzagged into the road then between parked cars, drawing the aim away from Ruth and Nathan.

He saw Nathan looking over at him, worried.

'Just keep running.'

They were already halfway to the bottom of the road. There was a downward slope driving them onwards, but it was doing the same for the guys behind.

A third pistol crack. Mark heard a fizz then a clunk as the bullet embedded itself in a parked Skoda.

He slalomed out on to the road then back in again.

He pulled at Ruth, who was lagging behind.

Up in front, Nathan staggered and fell.

Mark almost kicked him as he stumbled into him on the pavement. He clambered upright, dragged the boy by the arm on to his feet and pushed him on.

Crack.

Mark's heart was thumping, head pounding, lungs raw. He wondered about Ruth. She was ahead of them now as Mark urged Nathan forward, glancing behind.

They were still the same distance away.

They hit the bottom of the street and ran over to the prom.

'Head for the beach,' Mark shouted.

The streetlights along the prom were fizzing with sodium light. Low cloud scudded overhead. Wind in their faces. The clouds were orange with reflected light over the city, but dark grey out to sea. The tide was way out, three hundred yards of damp sand between the edge of the water and high tide.

No moon meant it was hard to see out there. Mark tried to follow the ribs of a wooden groyne, his eye running along the spine as it stretched towards the sea. But it got lost in a black fuzz before the water.

Hopefully they could lose Fisher and Blue in that darkness.

He couldn't hear the waves from here, the wind roaring in his ears.

He glanced along the prom as they got to the sand. No one. Mark headed left. 'This way.'

The dry sand under their feet sucked at their legs. Like wading. But it would be the same for the other two behind.

Then after twenty yards the sand was compacted, easier to run on.

They scrabbled over a ridge of seaweed, high tide, and Mark guided them into the darkness, further away from the glare of the lights on the prom.

Another look back. Fisher and Blue were standing on the prom, looking around. Frantic movements spotlit under a streetlamp.

They caught sight of Mark and headed towards the beach.

Mark backed away, still looking at Fisher and Blue.

A stench came to his nostrils.

He tripped and fell over something. Something big. It sent him reeling and tumbling, his face full of sand.

He lurched upright spitting sand and saw what it was.

A whale. A dead pilot whale. Its skin greasy in the half-light, its bulk ominous and alien.

The crack of a gun.

He flinched, turned and ran.

Then he saw the rest of them.

Dozens of dead whales, scattered all across the beach, stretching for several hundred yards at least, like sleeping giants. Their sleek, oily outlines looked like an invading army.

So they'd done it, they'd finally killed themselves.

Nathan and Ruth were holding hands ahead of him, darting in between the whales' bodies, zigzagging across the sand.

Mark propelled himself towards Ruth and the boy, into the encroaching darkness.

The smell was overpowering. Saltiness, ammonia and rotting meat clung to the back of his throat as he heaved in air and staggered forward.

He passed another dead whale, then another, the black eyes staring at him.

Nathan and Ruth were over a groyne up ahead.

Mark approached another whale corpse and spotted something. A piece of flotsam, a thick wooden slat from a packing crate, about the length of a baseball bat.

He picked it up, rough wood against his hands, and felt the heft of it.

It would do.

He sped on to the next whale, then skidded down behind it as he passed, pushed himself against the animal's skin, holding the slat in both hands.

The whale's body was hard and dry, like rubber. Not oily at all up close.

His heart was hammering in his throat, his pulse singing in his ears.

He hoped they hadn't seen him duck down.

He looked the other way. He couldn't make out Ruth or Nathan. Good. If he couldn't see them, Fisher couldn't either.

He had to bring this to an end. Had to protect what was left of his family.

Footsteps and breathing.

There was a scuff of sand kicked up, then Fisher was past, gun held out in front of him as he stumbled forward.

Then Mark heard Blue wheezing, almost at the whale.

He stepped out, lifting the slat back and swinging it with all his power into Blue's face.

Blue's cheek crumpled and burst open, his jaw caved in and teeth went flying. He collapsed on to his knees and swayed as Mark lifted the slat and whipped it across his face again, sending more teeth and blood spraying on to the sand, ripping his jaw away from his face on the near side. Blue slumped sideways and dropped the Browning.

Mark picked up the gun.

Fisher was turning round at the sound of the attack.

Mark pulled the trigger and Fisher span as a bullet caught him in the hip, a small spurt of blood at the entry wound.

Fisher fired his gun as he fell, way off balance.

Mark staggered back as a burning sensation spread through his left shoulder. The stench of gunpowder and blood was overpowering. Shot. His shoulder was on fire with pain, but he didn't fall down, just walked towards Fisher, lying in the wet sand.

Got to him in three strides and stamped on his gun hand, digging the heel of his foot in as hard as he could.

Fisher screamed and pulled his arm away, leaving the gun behind in the sand. He shuffled backwards, clutching at his hip, glistening with blood.

Mark tried to pick the gun up with his injured arm, made a grimace. He had no power, couldn't move his fingers for the pain shooting through his body. Instead he kicked the gun away across the sand.

He pointed the Browning at Fisher. Had the urge to squeeze the trigger. Felt the pain sweeping along his left arm, swarming into his body. Glanced down at the wound. A fucking mess.

He looked at Blue. Out cold on the beach. Like a miniature version of one of the whales.

Turned back to Fisher.

'Don't,' Fisher said.

'Give me a reason not to.'

Fisher swung his leg round across the surface of the sand and caught Mark on the calf, sweeping him off his feet. The Browning flew out of Mark's hand, somewhere out into the dark, and he landed with a thump on his back.

Fisher scrambled over, clutching his hip, leaking blood. He punched Mark on his injured shoulder, making him howl and squirm.

Fisher was on him now, throwing punches at his face and shoulder. Mark tried to push him off but he had no energy left. With each punch he was losing the fight, the pain soaking into his bones and sapping his strength. He took another hit to the shoulder then one to the face and felt a tooth come loose and slip down his throat. There was blood in his mouth and nose and his eye was closing up. He held his good hand up to stop the blows but Fisher was much stronger, despite the bullet in the hip, and he punched through Mark's hand as if it wasn't there.

Crack.

A spray of blood sputtered out the side of Fisher's head. He sat there for a moment looking surprised, then fell on top of Mark in an awkward embrace.

Mark heaved him off and turned.

Ruth stood a few feet away, eyes glazed, pointing the gun. A smudge of smoke curled up from its barrel.

Mark checked Fisher's body. Small entry wound on his right temple, large exit wound on the left-hand side of his skull.

Mark hauled himself over and up on to his knees, spitting blood on to the sand.

'Where's Nathan?'

Ruth didn't move.

'Ruth?'

She lowered the gun then nodded behind Mark.

Mark turned and saw the boy emerge from behind a dead whale fifty feet away, face white against the darkness, as if he was a source of light himself.

Mark looked at Blue. Still out cold, his jaw and part of his ear hanging off. Maybe dead.

He turned back to Nathan and struggled to his feet.

'Come on, Big Guy. It's OK. It's safe now.'

Nathan crept towards Mark and Ruth, like he was sneaking out of bed after lights out.

Mark raised a hand to his beaten face, blood and swelling across his eye and cheek. Then he beckoned Nathan.

Nathan began jogging, then running, then he launched himself into Mark's embrace. Mark got a jolt of pain at the contact, his shoulder pulsing blood out the wound.

Nathan threw a look at Fisher and Blue.

'Are the bad men dead, Daddy?'

Mark wasn't sure about Blue, but it was too complicated to go into.

'Yes, they're dead.'

'Did Gran shoot one of them?'

Mark looked at Ruth, still dazed, gun held loose in her hand. 'Yes, she did.'

'Just like I shot the man at home?'

'That's right.'

'But it wasn't bad, what we did, was it?'

Mark knelt down and put a hand to the boy's cheek. Tears and snot there, his eyes red. Mark thought about what those eyes had seen, what had soaked into the boy's mind. Unbearable, like everything else.

'Listen to me, Big Guy. What you did wasn't bad at all. You saved Daddy, remember that. And Gran did the same thing. She saved both of us from the bad men, OK?'

Nathan looked unsure for a moment, then nodded, but there wasn't much conviction in it.

'Jesus.' It was Ferguson, out of breath, feet slapping up to them.

She stopped and got her breath back, bent over with her hands on her thighs.

She looked round and took in the scene. After a while she spoke.

'Armed response unit is on its way.'

'Where's the kid cop?' said Mark.

Ferguson pointed towards Marlborough Street. 'He's got Mr Taylor.'

Mark nodded.

Ferguson approached Ruth and put a hand out for the gun. 'I'll take that, Mrs Bell.'

Ruth handed it over.

Ferguson scouted round and spotted Fisher's gun. Picked it up by the barrel. Then went over to Mark and looked at his shoulder and face.

'We'd better get an ambulance.'

There was a moan. Blue raised a hand to his mashed face, then the hand dropped on to the sand. His eyes remained closed.

'For him as well.'

Mark was still holding on to Nathan, the boy's shivering body against his chest.

'Can I take him away from here?'

Ferguson nodded. 'I'll call an ambulance, you three wait on the prom.'

Mark, Nathan and Ruth trudged across the sand, not looking back.

Behind them, Ferguson sighed. 'Christ, what a mess.'

40

The armed response unit turned up in a bluster of flashing lights and shouting, guys in bulletproof gear clumping around and pointing rifles.

Mark was slumped against the wall next to Ruth, his good arm pulling Nathan close. He pointed a thumb in the direction of the beach, then heard a crackle on one officer's walkie-talkie, Ferguson's tinny voice saying something he couldn't make out.

Mark felt Nathan tense at the sight of all the police, and held on tight.

The officers stomped across the sand, leaving one silent guy watching over the three of them, rifle at ease.

After a few minutes, another police van trundled along the prom. Guys in white overalls jumped out with bags of gear and headed for the beach.

Where the hell was the ambulance?

With the adrenalin ebbing away, Mark started to feel faint from the pain in his shoulder. Should he press something against it, stop the bleeding? That's what they did in the movies.

He breathed through clenched teeth, concentrated on the molecules of air coming and going, mingling with his bloodstream and keeping him alive.

Then at last an ambulance.

'Thank fuck.' Under his breath so Nathan didn't hear.

Two paramedics checked him out, gave him a painkilling injection and fussed him into the back of the ambulance.

'These two come as well,' he said.

Ruth and Nathan clambered up and sat next to him. Mark held on to Nathan and looked at Ruth. She put on a weak smile. She still hadn't spoken since she'd shot Fisher.

Ferguson came over as a second ambulance appeared, and she pointed the medical team towards the beach, where Blue was lying. The paramedics scuttled off with a stretcher and an oxygen mask.

Ferguson turned to Mark. She had a thin smile on her face.

'When you're sorted, DI Green and I will need to talk to you at the station.'

'Fine.'

'All three of you.'

Mark sighed. 'I want to keep Nathan out of it as much as possible.'

Ferguson nodded and closed the ambulance doors.

41

'Can I get a story, Daddy?'

All those years of sticking to the bedtime book routine. Even now, with the afternoon sun bleaching in through closed curtains.

Mark tucked Nathan up into his and Lauren's bed and stroked the boy's mess of hair.

'Sure, Big Guy, what would you like?'

'*What Was I Scared Of?*, please.'

Still saying please and thank you, despite it all. A polite, well-balanced boy. We done good with this one, Lauren, we done good. Another little joke between them, a line they trotted out in a hokey hillbilly accent every time they took a cute photo of him. Another little joke lost to the world.

Mark reached the same bit in the story that always got to him – large, dark double page, a bleak, apocalyptic landscape. Two frightened white eyes staring out. Those insistent words, the ones that killed him, about being truly afraid and lying about it.

Nathan's eyes were already closed. Not quite asleep, but on the way. Mark was struck again by the resilience of kids, of his boy in particular. The elasticity of them, stretching and bending with whatever the world hurled at them, not letting it break them. He felt brittle in contrast, like an ancient tomb ready to crumble into dust at the slightest touch.

He stroked Nathan's head for a few minutes, then noticed the dry lips. Reached for the Vaseline and rubbed some on. Thought about Lauren's lips. Always thinking about that beneath it all.

He rose slowly from the bed then snuck out the door. The boy hadn't slept since the break-in. Mark hoped he would have good dreams, but didn't know if there was much chance of that.

He left the room and went to the kitchen. Ruth sat at the table, a cup of tea gone cold in front of her, untouched. She was staring out the window. The clutter of beech trees was still, their leaves soaking in the sunshine. The wind had finally given up, the storm blowing itself out.

Mark sat down and placed a hand on top of Ruth's. Felt the looseness of her skin again. He would never feel Lauren's hand like that, slack on the bone with age.

Ruth turned to him. The mundanity of the last few hours had seen the shock ebb away, replaced by deep sadness and resignation on her face.

'Will we be all right?' she said.

She meant with the police, not anything else. There was no answer to that other question.

They had told the truth. No point trying to cover up for Nathan and the corpse in the flat. Mark had explained everything – the break-in, the brothel, Taylor, Fisher. Thankfully, Taylor was backing up Mark's version of events, more or less. With Fisher dead, he wasn't scared for his life any more. He was playing down his role in it all, obviously, and was playing up the getting shot in the shoulder part. Mark wondered what would happen to Taylor, if he would be punished enough. He wondered what Taylor's wife would make of it all.

And he wondered about himself, whether he was going to go to prison for what he'd done. Always more stuff to worry about, it was never-ending. His son and mother-in-law had both shot and killed people to save his life. Ferguson's boss couldn't say for now if either of them would end up in court. If they did, they could claim self-defence, surely. But then Mark had read plenty of newspaper stories about people who shot burglars and did time for it. And of course, things were worse for Mark. He had shot someone, plain and simple, no self-defence about it. DI Green thought there might be scope for a deal with Taylor, but that was up in the air.

Mark had used a laptop at the police station to download the files Lauren had emailed to herself, passed them on to the cops. They had specialists looking at them. What they found would have a bearing on Taylor and everything else, but that would take time to work out.

In the meantime social services would have to investigate. Mark still had that playground assault charge hanging over him. Christ.

He realised he hadn't answered Ruth.

'We'll be fine, we'll look out for each other.'

He squeezed her hand, but it didn't feel like a comforting gesture, more like he was the one seeking reassurance.

He got up and went through to the living room. Forensics had removed the body after several hours fussing over the scene. Left behind was a huge pool of congealing blood. Ferguson had explained at the station that it wasn't the police's job to clear up. There was a specialist company they could hire in, but they cost £300 an hour. No chance. He'd have to do it himself. Towels, bucket, bleach, mop.

The imprint of the dead guy's body was still at the centre of the pool. The blood had run all the way to the skirting boards. Soaked in between the floorboards. They were never going to get it all out, it would haunt them as long as they stayed here, along with everything else.

'Should we make a start on it?' It was Ruth behind him. 'It'll only be harder to clean up later if we leave it.'

Mark rubbed at his swollen eye. Then stroked his shoulder, now wrapped in tight bandages. Apparently the wound was simple and clean, didn't take much at the hospital to patch it up. They'd given him three blister packs of codeine, and he'd swallowed four pills on the way to the police station with Nathan and Ruth.

He looked at the time. Almost three o'clock. School would be coming out soon.

'I'll get some things,' Ruth said.

And so they cleaned. As Nathan slept, Ruth worked the mop and Mark spread old towels out to soak everything up. Slow going for him with only one functioning arm, but after an hour or so they were down to scrubbing the floorboards and bleaching everything. They had the windows wide open to get rid of the smell. There had been some shit and piss as well, the guy's body slackening as he decomposed. The man had broken into their home, beaten Mark, threatened to kill him, tried to hurt Nathan, and here they were cleaning up his shit.

After another hour most signs were gone. There was nothing they could do about the gaps between the floorboards. Their eyes and hands were stinging from the bleach. They'd done enough for now.

Mark carried the cleaning stuff through to the kitchen and put it away. When he came back Ruth was lying on the sofa with her eyes closed and her hand on her forehead.

'I might just have forty winks,' she said.

Mark got a blanket and spread it over her, then he looked out the window at the old church across the road. It was a beautiful day outside, crisp and warm, one of those late spring days that give you a taste of approaching summer.

'I think I'll go for a walk,' he said.

Ruth opened her eyes. 'Really?'

'I need some air.'

'Don't be long. Nathan might wake up.'

He went to the front door.

'Daddy?'

He turned and saw Nathan at the bedroom door in another pair of those jammies that were too small for him.

'Where are you going?'

'Just out for a walk, Big Guy.'

'I want to come.'

'No, go back to sleep.'

'I want to go and see the whales,' Nathan said. 'Can we?'

Mark leaned against the door. 'Sure. Go and get dressed.'

He fingered the broken lock on the front door while he waited. Something else on the list of things to fix.

42

The beach was chaos.

Environmental health vans, coastguard vehicles, police cars and fire engines were all on the prom. Three news-crew vans were parked further along. Mark could see one reporter interviewing someone in a luminous yellow jacket, while the BBC woman was doing a piece to camera, the backdrop of the beach behind.

The whales were the story.

Mark, Ruth and Nathan's little adventure hadn't made it to the news yet. Ferguson said forensics had done a quick, clean job down on the sand, and it was assumed by early dog walkers and joggers that the police cordon was for the whales.

But their story would get out soon. Two men killed in Portobello on a single night. Two more with gunshot wounds. Another one in intensive care. The guy in the blue hoodie was alive. He was still heavily sedated because of his injuries. Mark might well be charged for that too, depending on what the guy had to say when he came round. Mark wondered if he was really the one who killed Lauren, like his partner had said. For all it mattered now.

For the moment, Mark, Ruth and Nathan had all been released without charge, but they'd been warned the situation might change. Just another thing to deal with in the coming days and weeks. For the rest of their lives. There would be press intrusion. He thought about the *Daily Record* journalist from yesterday. There might be court cases. There would be a funeral and counselling and grief and horror and nightmares and sorrow.

But not just now.

For now the beached whales were the story.

A crowd had gathered around the cordon, swollen by schoolkids let out of Towerbank, their red uniforms flashing between the grown-ups as they jostled to see.

Mark traipsed on to the sand and joined them, Nathan gripping his hand tight, staying close. There were forty-two whales, he heard an official saying to a reporter. The largest mass beaching ever recorded on Scottish shores. No one knew why. People never knew why. Sometimes bad things just happened.

Someone next to Mark mentioned the stench. All Mark could smell was bleach and blood.

How do you get rid of forty-two whales?

Mark thought about himself and Ruth scrubbing away at the floorboards in the flat.

He guided Nathan to a different part of the crowd, drifting round the outside. He spotted someone from the picture desk at the *Standard* snapping away. One of the new kids, eager to please and willing to work for next to nothing. He looked at the shot the guy was taking, it was all wrong, you'd get much better depth and contrast from further round. He tried to imagine taking pictures again, going back to work.

Mark and Nathan stood looking at the whales for a long time.

Eventually Nathan spoke.

'Where was Mummy found?'

Mark looked at him. 'What?'

'Where did they find Mummy?'

Mark turned and pointed in the other direction. 'Over there.'

'Can we go?'

'Why?'

'I want to see.'

'There's nothing to see.'

Nathan shrugged. 'I just want to.'

Mark thought for a long moment, looking at Nathan. Then he shrugged too.

'Come on.'

They walked away from the dead whales and the people and the noise and headed along the beach.

They climbed across a groyne, Mark lifting Nathan up and over the weathered wood, the pair of them heading for where Lauren had been washed up.

Mark saw her face clearly, marbled blue skin, pale lips, straggly hair.

They got to where it was and stopped.

'Here?' Nathan said.

Mark nodded. 'I think so.'

He glanced the way they'd come. The whales looked like little rocks from here, nothing more.

He turned back. They were close to the water's edge, ten feet. It was calm out in the firth, the sun bouncing on the flat surface like hammered tin.

Nathan was scuffing in the sand with his shoe. Mark wondered what was going through his head.

The boy went into his pocket and took something out. It was the piece of sea glass. He sat down on the sand and dug a small hole. Put the glass in the hole and covered it over.

'Don't you want to keep that?' Mark said.

Nathan shook his head. 'I'm showing it to Mummy like I wanted to.'

Mark sat down next to Nathan and pulled him into a hug.

'I'm sure Mummy loves it,' he said.

He sat there holding the boy, looking out to sea, trying not to think of anything at all.

Acknowledgements

Huge thanks to Angus Cargill, Katherine Armstrong, Eleanor Rees, Hannah Griffiths, Alex Holroyd, Lisa Baker, Sam Brown, John McColgan and everyone else at Faber for their continued belief and support. Thanks also to fellow writers Allan Guthrie and Helen FitzGerald for inspiration and sound advice. And the biggest thanks to Trish, for putting up with it all.